Thanks to

Steve, Rhys, Elinor, Jess and Tash

Dear Reader, Welcome to my third book, which I thank you for buying.

I hope this will make you laugh as I found it great fun to write it.

Thanks to my friends who over the years after a drink or two, have shared our disastrous stories. I found that sharing your stories with your mates make it seem not so bad.

So I hope this book will be good to read to take your mind off flying in a plane or waiting in the dentist, or a train journey at night where there is no view. Anytime you need to relax, laugh and appreciate life.

Also I found that when my children left home I did feel lost. Chatting and sharing with my friends we realised we were going through the same thing. But luckily it does pass, there is life after kids. That's why I started to write books to fill the gaps with my time.

Well I have to get on got I have another book to write. Lol.

See you in the next book.

Jo Jo x

And Then There Were TWO.....

By Josephine Jones

CHAPTER 1

EMPTY NEST

Megan parked her new black Audi A3 in the garage and made her way to her four bedroom detached house, her family's home. This house that use to be so warm and welcoming, which had always been a thing of pride and filled her with joy. Now Megan felt had been replaced with a cold lonely vacuum.

Her anxiety began as soon as she woke up this morning filled with trepidation about going home to an empty house. She was reluctant to leave work and her colleagues, engaging them in inane light hearted chatter to delay the evitable return home. She took a deep breath, put the key in the door and opened it.

The first thing she noticed was the colourful Italian tiles she had scoured the internet for. There were no bags or coats, no shoes strewn across the hall. These obstacles that used to irritate her making her vocally chastise the children were now gone. She slowly removed her jacket hanging it on the coat hook that despite her endeavours were completely ignored by her children. While placing her shoes in the shoe rack, she was suddenly hit by the silence. She held on to the oak banister to look upstairs, there was no music, or rather the noise that the kids insisted was music, to assault her ears. In the living room the television off, this was unheard off. The television was always on and always seemed to be playing to an empty room, whenever Megan returned home from work much to her annoyance. Of course when challenged the kids insisted they were watching it. She walked along the polished oak floor into the living room, the television seemed dark and imposing now, fixed to the wall looking out of place in her immaculate Venetian style living room.

Why mused Megan had there been such a desperate need to place a modern monstrosity of a 51 inch screen over her beautiful marble fireplace and why had she deemed it necessary to spend four thousand pounds on that settee? No longer was there a PlayStation being played in the kitchen diner. She had spent many a tortuous hour designing a games corner so that the children could still been seen even though cosseted in their own world. Most of all there was no arguing, no tears, no laughter in fact thought Megan thought no life.

It seemed to Megan as if her home had turned into a soulless catacomb. She could even hear her own breathing it was so deathly quiet. She sat on the kitchen stool and cried, all the things that the kids use to do that were so wearing and frustrating were gone and she missed them.

You should be happy, she chastised herself, *they were not dead, they were leading happy independent lives isn't this is what parenthood is all about? Of course it is, job well done Mrs Jones. Bringing up and nurturing three well-adjusted human beings to this mad unforgiving world.*

So why, thought Megan, *am I feeling so low and so alone. Where have I gone wrong? What's wrong with me, for Christ sake!*

Megan stopped crying and put the kettle on. Her mother always had tea on the go for visitors, not only to quench a thirst but a cure for any shock or illness and a lubricant for conversation. She smiled as she fondly remembered her mum, ever resourceful, there was no problem that could not be sorted out over a cup of tea. Taking her china cup and saucer she sat down in her mother's old rocking chair looking over her perfectly manicured garden through a wall of glass and savoured the tea. God how she missed her mum, when she left university with a degree in politics and economics she felt completely lost. She had been on the rollercoaster of academia then sudden was released into the real world, to find a "career."

It was her ever practical mum who suggested she apply for the job of school secretary, at the local primary school where she worked as the cook.

"Just to tide you over love, until you know what you want to do," that was the wisdom she had imparted.

Megan smiled to herself looking towards the heavens, *God that was 30 years ago mum and I 'm still there at St Anne's Primary School. Where had the time gone? What have I done with my life all these years?*

As the darkness descended on the October evening Megan caught sight of her reflection in the patio window. There was a frumpy overweight woman staring back at her that she did not recognise. This unwanted vision made her stand up hurriedly to blot it out. Instead focused on the job in hand, preparing her husband's tea.

She rinsed out her cup and placed it with the saucer into the dishwasher. She removed her blue cardigan and busily put on her clean apron. Her mother being a cook would instil into Megan that only "sluts" cooked without an apron, after many instances of exploding sauces, Megan reluctantly agreed with her. Although now her clothes were a uniform of black top and trousers with an assortment of coloured cardigans that her mother had bought her over many Christmases. She still felt naked without an apron on when cooking. She switched on the radio and pulled her everyday ponytail into a makeshift bun. She washed her hands and determinedly set about making a casserole for her husband's tea.

Her cooking skills always seemed inferior to her mums. Her mums cooking of course was legendary but had not hesitated to give up this up to look after her husband, Peter Cassagrande.

He was a second generation Portuguese immigrant who had always worked hard as a bricklayer unfortunately by a cruel turn of fate, at the age of 40 was struck down with Motor Neurone Disease. Two years of dedicated caring for her husband came to an end when he peacefully passed away at home in his bed from a stroke.

Megan's mum did not have the heart to return to work as the stress of being such a selflessly dedicated nurse, who had willingly neglected her own health had taken its toll. She also became a heavy smoker when her husband became ill, but then who could begrudge her only pleasure left in life.

Even so her house always remained open to all and she always seemed to have a lodger of some sort or another and cooked for anyone who called. She was a dedicated free childminder for Megan and conveniently she had lived right by the primary school for which Megan had been eternally grateful for.

One by one the children grew up negating a need for a childminder as they left to attend secondary school.

Megan's life became very busy looking after teenagers and time to visit her mum became more difficult to find. Partly because of this Megan did not discover her mother had bowel cancer until it had reached an advanced stage. This cancer which had viscously, stealth fully and without conscious took her mum from her. Megan didn't know how long her mum had been ill. Her mum Gwendoline never complained, she was always so excited when Megan visited her, making her feel guilty that she did not pop over more often, she always left her mums vowing to be a better daughter but always seemed to fail. The children came and went as they pleased. But Gwendoline still made them feel welcome and wanted to know everything about their lives for those few minutes making them they were the centre of the universe. She gave unconditional love along with cake and tea. She was always bursting with pride for her family, who could do no wrong in her eyes.

Even Paul Megan's husband loved visiting "Mrs C" as her friends knew her, a name she got when she was the school cook, as the children use to find Cassagrande hard to say and called her Mrs "C" instead, and so it stuck much to her amusement.

Paul would boast how he had the best mother in law in the world which of course made Gwen light up with sheer delight.

Megan's husband and children loved Gwen's cooking, especially her welsh cakes. Megan humbly accepted she did not have her mother's culinary skills. She had the gift of being able to make a meal out of anything. It was no surprise that her eldest son Iestyn would follow in his Nana's footsteps and happily went off to catering college and is now a much acclaimed chief in a restaurant in Brighton.

Oh mum you would be so proud, thought Megan as she guiltily added a packet mix to the casserole.

Megan had been thrilled with Iestyn's passion for cooking and had proudly (and gratefully) stood down from the cooking duties for a while. They had even painstakingly designed the kitchen together and with Iestyn's influence had every gadget under the sun. All her friends and family were in awe of such a well-equipped and organized fabulous kitchen that only an OCD chief could design. In fact Megan was intimidated by its splendour, she felt that her cooking did not measure up to her impeccable surroundings. This of course did not detract from the immense pride she had for her son every time she stepped in there.

Megan glanced at the clock, just past 6 O 'clock, yes she could allow herself a glass of red wine. She always felt that the "Floyd" way of cooking and drinking helped her cope with her continual disappointment in her efforts. She laid the table for two and roughly cut the fresh bread she had bought from her local bakery on her way to work this morning. She changed the music to Bach to try and ease her pain away. She removed her apron sat at the table and let the wine and music flow through her veins.

At seven o'clock Megan heard Paul's silver Mercedes C Class pull up outside. By the time he entered the kitchen he had already removed his jacket and replaced it with his comfy grey cardigan and slippers.

He smiled kissing Megan on the cheek as their usual greeting,

"Hi Meg, had a good day?"

Megan smiled back at her husband and replied the automatic response of,

"Yes of course, how was your day?"

She poured out a glass of wine for him while Paul told Megan all about his day.

"That Dubai trip has paid off, a chain of hotels in London are interested now….."

Megan smiled and made the polite responses at the appropriate times while serving a plate of hot casserole and continued to listen as she served herself and sat down to eat.

Paul was one of six children and had joined the Fire Service at eighteen. His parents were not well off and could not afford to support him in university. He later went on to university as a mature student with Megan's unwavering support. He not only achieved a degree but went on to complete a masters too. He then setup his own risk assessment consultancy, his name Paul Jones was well known and his company "Salus" (after the roman goddess of safety and wellbeing) was in great worldwide demand for its knowledge of Health and Safety and he was regularly invited to present on the subject at major conferences.

As Megan and Paul ate silence fell at the table as Beethoven softly serenaded their meal. Megan looked at the man she had been married to for twenty five years and had three children by. *Where had the man that had dark thick hair and was crazy about her? They used to laugh, gosh she could not remember the last time she had laughed. Are you happy Paul?* She thought to herself, looking at his serious face. Then pushed the scary thought away. *She couldn't cope with that answer. Why was she tormenting herself with these thoughts*?

Megan looked again at her husband although he had lost his hair he still looked handsome and trim, his early morning swims helped him to manage that. He was respected and had a successful company which suddenly made her irrationally jealous and annoyed at him.

How is it that men looked great without hair? She said to herself in dismay.

Megan had never had time to keep fit, she was not only a full time school secretary she also acted as the headmaster Mr Evans' personal assistant. Mr Evans still had the same greasy hair with the same side parting that he had since he was a schoolboy which was complimented by Dandruff over the shoulders of his only suit.

He obviously thought this look was attractive to women as she had spent the first 10years of her job being chased around the desk avoiding his advances.

*Christ even **his** unwanted advances had stopped,* she suddenly realised. *When did that happen? Had she become that unattractive?* She quickly sipped her wine to try to dispel that thought.

Megan knew that she ran the school and all its events like clockwork, she smiled sipping the wine self-assured. She also was a parent/ teacher mediator as she had known most of the people in the village for years she had become an unofficial family counsellor. The weight of knowing everyone's secrets had made her more wary of what she could share with to Paul, so limiting their topics of conversation. She became a good listener, unfortunately over the years had made her form the habit of being reluctant to talk when she got home.

"That was lovely Megan," said Paul pushing his empty plate gently away as he sat back and drank his wine.
"Thank you."

Megan smiled knowingly in return of his polite praise for her cooking efforts. He never complained, he had always encouraged the children to give the same platitudes. She quietly got up and collected the dishes, rinsed them and placed them in the dishwasher.

On finishing her chores she looked around and suddenly noticed Paul had left his seat and had settled in front of the television to watch the latest David Attenborough documentary.

Megan sighed and suddenly feeling exhausted explained to Paul that she was tired and would go to bed to read.

"Ok love, night" replied Paul not taking his eyes off the television.

Megan, released from her role of dutiful wife, headed upstairs.

The children's bedroom doors were shut tight. Megan did not want to venture into them as they were still filled with posters, toys and other precious possessions. It would make the children's absence even more unbearable. She had cleaned and tidied Iestyn's room, then shut it up ready for his infrequent visits home. She had slowly gone through the same process for Angharad's room when she left to go to Bath University to do Sports Science. Angharad had always been sport mad, she was always out with one club or another. Her and her dad had extensively travelled Britain following Cardiff City. But last summer she went travelling around Canada with her friend Brock.

"I'm too busy having a great time to come home mum" she said but promised a compensatory visit at Christmas.

Now it's Lloyd's turn. Megan wasn't expecting him to go to university, he had never been interested in school. Megan was secretly relieved that her youngest might stay home

but alas, it wasn't to be. He was off to Newcastle University to do a degree in Economics, Philosophy and

Politics. Paul had been so proud of Lloyd's amazing A level results but Megan had been in shock and denial.

Newcastle for Christ sake! Could he have gone any further away from his home in South Wales? Did he hate this beautiful home that she had painstakingly created? She thought as she angrily brushed her teeth.

When she saw the blood in the sink she knew she was getting carried away. She rinsed her toothbrush slowly and deliberately replaced it in the silver holder. She calmly rinsed with the strong minty mouthwash and smiled at her reflection to check her teeth.

There she thought, *my teeth are fine and so am I.*

She entered her luxurious bedroom, switching on the expensive chandelier light fitting that she bought in Paris. She made her way across the warm thick pile cream carpet, past her walk-in wardrobe, to close the damask gold curtains. Slowly she removed her clothes and placed them in the laundry hamper. She put on her thick warm cotton pyjamas and made her way to the ornate dressing table. Sitting on the cream satin stool she ritually cleansed and moisturised her face and hands, then slowly went to her king-sized oak sleigh bed removing the artfully arranged cream and gold cushions (that in her opinion made the room look so sumptuous) and placed them into the ottoman at the end of the bed. She pulled back the satin throw and white duvet to reveal the inviting crisp white sheets and thankfully climbed into bed.

The day was nearly over and she had survived, she thought.

She picked up her kindle to read but the relief was short lived as tears slowly trickled down her cheeks as she in realising that the next day would soon be here.

Megan was already awake and staring at the ceiling when the alarm clock went off. Paul opened his eyes and stretched over to stop the alarm which then started playing the radio. He got out of bed and put on his sweat shirt, swimming trunks and jogging bottoms. He smiled at Megan, who was now sat up in bed, he leaned over kissing her cheek saying his ritual "Good morning "

Then he picked up his kitbag and left for his morning swim. Megan slowly made her way to the shower to lather herself

in her lavender and Jasmin shower gel and coconut shampoo and conditioner. She dried herself in her Egyptian cotton towels wrapping her long dark greying hair in a towel.

She mindlessly walked into her wardrobe and pulled out her black top, trousers and sensible beige underwear and got dressed. Then arduously finished drying her thick uncontrollable wavy hair with her hair dryer.

"I can't remember the last time I went to the hairdressers." She sighed to herself.

She made her way wearingly downstairs, Paul had switched the coffee machine on for her so she emptied the dishwasher putting everything back in their rightful place. She drank her coffee and ate her granola at the breakfast bar alone listening to the radio. When finished rinsed her cup and bowl and put them in the dishwasher.

She had never felt as lonely before as she made her way to their bedroom and carefully remade the bed dutifully replacing the cushions in their allotted position. The immaculate bedroom gave her no satisfaction today. Paul had often joked to friends that he was too scared to make the bed as it would make him late for work and never redo it to Megan's standard so if she was away he would sleep on the settee. She had laughed along at the time but now stood alone gazing at the bed and wondered,

How many a true word is said in jest. When did they stop having sex , Christ when was the last time they had even touched each other aside from the obligatory peck on the cheek. Was it when she had created this showpiece bedroom or before?

She went back to the bathroom to clean her teeth and rinsed her mouth again with mouthwash. As she stared into the bathroom mirror she said determinedly,

"This has got to change, this is not living, and I'm just a machine carrying out daily tasks. What the hell am I going to do to change things?"

She made her way back downstairs put her coat and shoes on and as she grabbed her bag she suddenly realised she was drowning in her own solitude and self-pity. Things needed to change drastically in her life for her to survive.

CHAPTER 2

THE MAKEOVER

It was lunchtime and Megan was still pondering how to kick start her life. Billie plonked herself onto Megan's desk stretching out her long slim legs, her half Somalian heritage giving them a lovely natural tan. Billie who was unmarried with no children was a newly qualified teacher who had only been in the school for a year. Megan and Billie hit it off as soon as they met and it felt they had known each other for years. Billie had always hinted that Megan should go out more but seemed quite happy with meeting up for the odd coffee and chat in work.

"What's up Megan, are you missing Lloyd that badly?" she asked concerned.

"Is it that obvious? "Megan asked feeling a little unnerved.

"Well I did pull the short straw as everyone is worried about you" Billie explained softly.

"Everyone!" Megan gasped in horror.

"Yes everyone" stated Billie. "You are going around with a face like a slapped arse! So do you blame them?"

"Oh I am so sorry. I just feel so, so lost" explained Megan relieved to have found the right word. *Yes I am lost* she thought.

Megan the mum was gone. Megan the ragdoll with no purpose is left.

She added in despair, "The children took all my life and energy with them when they left home."

"But Megan, isn't this is a great opportunity to rediscover yourself. Weren't you complaining to me just the other day that you haven't had your hair done for years?"

"I can't remember that last time I had my hair done" cried out Megan tears running down her cheeks.

Megan was feeling a like child unable to cope. Megan the organised, Megan the professional was now Megan the blubbering mess. Billie rushed over and gave her a cwtch, unfortunately at that moment Mr Evans opened Megan's door to witness this emotional scene. Billie waved him away, embarrassed he quietly apologised, leaving the room closing the door gently behind him.

"Hey chin up love, Auntie Billie is going to be your fairy godmother" cooed Billie as she rubbed Megan's back.

This coming from a 25year old made Megan laugh hysterically, which in turn made Billie laugh too.

"What am I going to do?" laughed Megan wiping away the tears with the tissues she kept for parents and teachers alike. She was usually the good listener rather than the one pouring her heart out. This feeling of helplessness was totally alien to Megan.

"Right then" said Billie taking control. "I am going to ring my hairdresser and see if she has an appointment this afternoon."

"That's ok" said Megan in a daze "Paul's in London for a few days."

"Look, sod Paul we are going to look after you now love, ok" said Billie determinedly.

"Ok" said Megan trying her best to be positive but really was panicking inside.

"Don't worry, you're only going to have your haircut, anyone would think I was taking you to the Guillotine" said Billie reassuringly.

Megan nodded her head while blowing her nose and tried to force a smile to show Billie she was ok.

"I'll go and make you a lovely cup of tea" said Billie unconvinced, as she left the office.

Now alone Megan attempted to pull herself together. She went down the corridor to the ladies and washed her face and brushed her long thick wavy hair.

What am I letting herself in for? She anxiously thought.

She made her way back to her office feeling a little better to find a very pregnant Jayne with a tray holding a cup of tea and a couple of pieces of Bara brith.

"Billie sent me in with this, as she is busy on the phone" said Jayne as she put down the tray on the desk and struggled to sit down in the chair opposite. "How are you feeling?" asked Jayne gently.

"Oh I'm fine thanks" said Megan brushing away the concern, seeing Jayne in such discomfort brought out the mother in Megan regaining her composure. "More importantly how are you?"

"Oh can't wait to finish to be honest "confided Jayne as sat wide legged rubbing her enlarged stomach. "It's only Seren's amazing Bara brith that's keeping me going." She laughed.

"When are you finishing?" asked Megan

"As soon as they can get the supply teacher organised. The agency is as useless as a chocolate teacup to be honest. They're messing Mr Evans around terribly."

"Well let's hope they sort it out soon, otherwise I'll be delivering this baby!" exclaimed Megan sipping her tea. "Ah this tea is lush, thanks lovely."

No problem" said Jayne.

In rushed Billie, "It's all set!" she exclaimed. "Seren and I are taking you to have your hair done Saturday morning. Then we are taking you for a makeover, as Seren's friend works on a designer make up counter! And best of all, there is a sale on in the clothing dept. How fantastic is that!" screamed Billie excitedly.

"Well somewhat exciting" agreed Jayne smiling at Megan.

"Oh I don't know?" said Megan unsure.

"Oh Megan, what is there to worry about? You are going to be pampered all day, sounds great to me" said Jayne getting up from her chair.

"Don't think about it enjoy it!" said Billie a bit more controlled now.

"Oh ok" agreed Megan resignedly.

"Yes" said Jayne and Billie in unison and quickly kissed Megan on the cheek in turn and left the office.

"You won't regret it "whispered Billie as she left and in walked Mr Evans, coughing awkwardly and so the normal day's events resumed…………

On Saturday morning when Megan woke she was surprised at the excitement she felt. It was a lovely sunny morning and she enthusiastically sprang out of bed and had a quick shower, careful not to get her hair wet. She put on a pair of old faded jeans check shirt and old blue chunky cardigan, putting her hair in a ponytail and went downstairs. She switched on the radio, turning it up loudly to radio 1 rather than the usual radio 2, dancing around the kitchen making the coffee. Until some rapping song came on and she turned it quickly back to radio 2.

Mmm perhaps a step too far, she thought to herself laughing while pouring her usual granola into the bowl and sipped her coffee.

As she finished brushing her teeth, there was a knock at the door. Megan rushed to open the door to find Billie with her sleek jet black hair shining brightly in the sun. Billie theatrically removed her sunglasses to show her perfectly made up face which enhanced her natural beautiful. She wore a figure hugging body con patterned dress with her ankle boots showed off her long slender legs. The look was finished off with a denim Jacket.

"Are you ready darling" purred Billie with a cheeky wink.

"You look amazing" gasped Megan.

As Megan grabbed her basket weave bag, she realised how drab she must look compared to Billie.

"Thanks mate but it's you who is going to look amazing today. Come Cinderella your carriage awaits" giggled Billie as she ran towards Seren's bright yellow Volkswagen Beetle Cabriolet.

"Hi Megan, can you believe this weather? Isn't it wonderful!" shouted Seren blonde hair flowing as she lowered her sunglasses from her head to cover her eyes.

She wore a vest top and jeans using a floral blouse as a jacket.

"Yes" replied Megan getting in the car suddenly feeling warm which made her removed her comfy cardigan. "This is the perfect weather for your car."

"Yes it's hardly been a good weather this summer so roll on the Indian summer" added Billie as Seren sped off.

They were soon outside "Rose's Hair Salon," where they all disembarked from the car to begin their mission, "Operation Megan."

Megan's hair was soon being coloured and massaged in tropical smelling shampoo while they all excitedly drunk prosecco. Seren and Billie were pointing out articles from the magazines which prompted big discussions on the topics.

Megan could not believe how wonderful her hair felt after Rose had worked her magic. Her hair had been coloured warm chestnut to cover the encroaching grey. Then had been cut into a shaggy bob and serum applied allowing Megan's dark natural curls to return. Megan loved it as she felt lighter, younger more importantly attractive. She thanked Rose profusely.

Seren's husband Stuart had arrived to take them into town on to the next stage of their adventure. They made their way to the David Evans Department Store, where they were greeted by Seren's friend Siobhan at the makeup stand. She wore a medical looking white coat, her blonde hair was scraped into an immaculate bun to enhance of her perfect make up. Megan thought she looked the image of Queen Nefertiti, the sort of beauty attain if you are determined and work hard at it. Megan felt immediately inferior and lazy compared to all female kind, as she shyly sat on the stool offered,

"Hello Megan, Seren's told me so much about you" said Siobhan.

"She has?" questioned Megan surprised.

"Megan, what is your usual cleansing routine for your skin?" asked Siobhan getting straight to business.

"Routine for my skin?" Megan nervously questioned.

"Let's begin by finding out what do you use to wash your face in the morning?" Siobhan coaxed.

"Your daily routine" encouraged Billie.

"Well "said Megan thinking in desperation of something to say, "I suppose I use the antibacterial hand wash."

"Pardon!" cried Siobhan, as her colour drained from her face.

Even her foundation seemed to pale as she recoiled in utter horror.

Megan thought she would might just as well had said the blood from virgins such was the reaction she got from her.

"Oh Megan you do make me laugh!" cried Billie hanging onto Seren to keep herself from falling over with laughter.

Siobhan recovered herself from this shocking admission from Megan and said gently. "I am sorry Megan but you are stripping the goodness from your skin by using such a harsh substance on such a delicate skin."

"Oh" said Megan blushing with embarrassment.

"We will leave you be" said Billie wiping the tears of laughter from her eyes. "There is a café on the top floor, we'll wait for you there, Hun ok?"

"Ok "said Megan nervously thinking *like rats deserting a sinking ship.*

"Good, then I can concentrate on you" said Siobhan regaining her professional persona.

Siobhan kindly suggested that Megan could use a soap but was better off with a gentler one. She patiently cleansed Megan's face then toned and moisturised it while suggesting the new ritual she should adopt.

After this treatment Megan's skin felt revitalised. Siobhan then took out her own tweezers and proceeded to tidy up the stray hairs of her uncontrolled brows.

"You have a lovely natural shape to your brow Megan and you are lucky that thick eye brows are back in fashion. They just needed a little tidying to show off the shape."

She then patiently showed her how to apply the correct make up, in the correct order. At the end of the session Megan was handed a mirror to look at the results and she was amazed how good she looked. She gratefully bought the introduction skin cleansing kit and some foundation , which meant she got a free make up bag some free make up to start her off. Thanking Siobhan she hurried to join the girls at the café to show off her new look.

"Wow Megan you look great!" exclaimed Seren while Billie gave out a loud wolf whistle which made Megan glow with embarrassed joy. "You take a seat and I'll get you a coffee" said Seren as she jumped up offering Megan her chair.

"Oh no you have done so much already" protested Megan.

"Nonsense this is your day" insisted Seren.

Megan obediently sat down with Billie, she did not know if it had been the prosecco or the fantastic day she had but she felt giddy with excitement.

Seren bought some salad sandwiches and coffee for them all. They busily chatted and admired Megan's new look as they ate and Megan felt marvellous.

After lunch they headed for the clothes section, the good day continued as in the sale they found a black lace cocktail dress that was reduced from one hundred pounds to thirty pounds which fitted Megan perfectly. It flowed over and smoothed her lumps and bumps, showing off an hour glass figure that she never knew she had.

"Oh god Megan "whispered Billie in horror. "When did you last shave your legs?"

Megan looked down with shock and flushed with embarrassment, hurriedly explained "I only shave my legs for the two weeks we go on holiday. I wear trousers every day, so what's the point?"

"Doesn't Paul mind?" asked Seren hesitantly.

"No" said Megan flustered with tears filling up in her eyes "He likes me natural."

In reality she couldn't remember when Paul last saw her legs let alone notice that she hadn't shaved them.

"Kinky" said Billie in mock approval.

"Well "said Seren unsure. "You only have this beautiful body for a short time. If you look after it well then husbands won't stray. Don't you want to make an effort just for Paul? Even if you have given up, it might make you feel better, may be even sexier."

Megan walked back into the changing room and sat with her head in her hands.

Beautiful body who is she kidding. Have I given up? More importantly has Paul given up? Is this why we don't have sex? He is having sex with someone who can be bothered to shave her legs?

"Are you ok in there Meg?" asked Billie gently through the curtain.

"Yes, Yes of course" said Megan hurriedly wiping her eyes and removing the dress.

"Good, Look I have found some killer shoes!" exclaimed Billie pushing a pair of bright red heals around the curtain. "They would look brilliant on you."

"Oh my god!" exclaimed Megan "I don't know?"

"Come on Meg. You're a really sexy lady, so enjoy it, it won't last long. We'll soon have blue legs and saggy boobs. You have nice shapely legs so make the most of them" encouraged Seren. Then she poked her head around the other side of the curtain "Sorry Meg, I didn't mean to hurt your feelings. My mouth goes into action sometimes before my brain."

"She can be a heartless bitch but that why we love her hey Meg?" questioned Billie poking her head around to follow the shoes.

 "Please forgive me?" begged Seren.

"These have got 40% off?" said Billie waving the shoes temptingly.

"Ok, ok I forgive you Seren and I will buy the bloody shoes!" exclaimed Megan laughing and feeling lucky to have such good friends.

"Now bugger off! Can't a girl get some peace when she is changing?"

"Right "announced Billie giving Megan the shoes "Bags!"

Oh Christ will I have any money left thought Megan as she got dressed.

After being escorted around the bag dept. she quickly settled on a black patent clutch bag before her nerves gave way.

 While being driven home by Seren's husband, Patrick. Billie announced that the Glyndwr Hotel was having a cocktails and dancing evening. So they both insisted that Megan should go out with them to show off the new look. Megan reluctantly agreed.

As Megan got ready for the evening her bravado had gradually replaced by utter panic. She dutifully shaved her legs and even moisturised them. With relief she found a pair of tights without a ladder which calmed her nerves. But really she knew it was the large vodka and tonic she had poured herself which was largely responsible for her nerves being calmed.

Megan looked nervously at the reflection of this new woman that stood before her. This reignited the memory of the woman she forgot had existed. She looked like Megan Cassagrande again rather than the plain Mrs Jones she had become. As she admired her daring red shoes she smiled as she remembering her mother saying

"Red shoes no knickers!"

"Don't worry mum I've got my knickers on" Megan remarked to the heavens above. Although these days they were beige comfortable underwear, the days of wearing delicate lacy underwear were long gone she sighed.

Who is going to see my underwear anyway? Thought Megan sadly.

As Megan took the last of her drink and sprayed herself with the Chanel No5, that Paul had got her for Christmas, the duty free from his many trips. There was a beep of a horn.

"I wish you could see me now Paul" she said sadly to her reflection, then another beep of the horn made her quickly grab her clutch bag and ran downstairs, as quickly as her shoes would let her , to Seren and Billie waiting in a taxi shouting for her to come on.

As she got into the taxi the girls cheered.

Seren said "Thank god we thought you had chickened out!"

"After all you two have done for me today there was no chance of that" Megan said determinedly. This was greeted by wild cheers from Billie and Seren, off they went to the Glyndwr Hotel

.CHAPTER 3

COCKTAILS AND TROUBLE!

They were soon crossing a river on an ornate stone bridge, which lead through a parting in the forest revealing an imposing mock castle.

"We're here! Sang Billie.

"Oh my god, it's really posh! Do you really think we would be allowed in?" asked Megan nervously.

"Of course!" said Billie. "Seren got married here, flash bitch! I've always wanted to see inside."

"My father paid though" said Seren self-consciously reacting to Seren's jibe.

"Hey I was only joking man, I'm jealous really. If I got married here I'd be shouting about it from the rafters no mistake."

"Wow! You had your reception here" gushed Megan getting out of the taxi in awe of its grandness. "Your parent's rich then?"

"Well a bit I suppose" said Seren shyly.

"Come on then Megan!" said Billie sensing Seren's reluctance. "Let's party."

Bloody Hell thought Megan as she awkwardly hurriedly hobbled after Billie and Seren, in red heels that felt less sexy now. She felt more like Bambi on ice, rather than Sophia Loren. *Christ I'm too old for this!*

Billie walked effortlessly up the stone steps leading to the entrance in her 9inch heels and skin-tight black dress that she seemed to have been sprayed on her amazing sleek figure emphasizing her long legs. To Megan she oozed sex.

Seren looked beautifully sophisticated with her blonde hair put up in a chignon. She wore a simple designer black dress and her bare tanned legs were completed with a pair of very high gladiator sandals. She looked couture immaculate which made Megan feel more inferior and insecure.

Oh my god I am so out of my depth here she thought as she crossed the black and white tiled floor of the hotel reception feeling like a scared child at her first communion.

In the restaurant Megan looked up to the ceiling to see a sight to behold, it was blue with small lights which looked like stars sparkling in the sky, this was enhanced by a band playing soft jazz.

 Megan gaze was magnetically drawn to an attractive blonde young man in a dark suit standing at the bar. She felt his eyes following her which made her stomach turn over with excitement and her skin tingle. Megan tried to stay composed and aloof as she walked across the room to join

Seren at the free table that she had found.

Billie grabbed the cocktail menu and beckoned toward the young dark waiter.

"How can I serve you tonight ladies" he asked in a Russian sounding accent.

"Well, we'll have three Mojitos to start with "announced Billie.

"What's that?" asked Megan bemused.

"Oh don't worry Hun, you'll love it, it tastes all minty" explained Billie.

"This is such a lovely place Seren, your wedding must have been dreamy" said Megan.

"Aw thanks Meg, it was a lovely wedding, where did you get married?" asked Seren.

"Oh we got married in St Anne's church in the village." Megan laughed as she reminisced." I wore a meringue dress, because we all wanted to look like Princess Diana then. We had the reception in the village hall, nothing posh like this. My mother did all the catering of course with her colleagues from the school canteen" sighed Megan as she remembered how excited she was that day.

Paul looked so sexy in his suit. The white shirt and blue cravat made appear his eyes an even deeper blue, set off of course by his full head of dark hair. God how we loved each other then.

"Sounds lovely" said Seren earnestly.

The Mojitos were quickly finished,

"Oooh lets have Margarita's next" announced Billie.

When the waiter brought the drinks over, Billie took a sip

and brazening asked the waiter "What's your name then?"

"Albert" he replied politely.

"Why thank you Albert" said Billie openly flirting.

Albert didn't reply but gave Billie a wink as he walked away.

"Mmm this one's nice "said Megan relaxing the alcohol started to take effect. "These seem to get better the more of them you drink."

"Well Meg, I still can't get over what you told Siobhan from the makeup counter. When you said…. When you said….. When you said you washed you face in antibacterial hand wash. Well I thought she was going to have a coronary!" Billie managed to blurt through the laughter.

"Oh yes I nearly pissed myself, I was laughing sooo much!" added Seren.

"We love you Meg, you are just so…… Meg!" they laughed.

Megan found herself effortlessly joining in their contagious drunken laughter.

"Cheers, here's to Meg, let's hope she never changes!" they toasted and knock back yet another cocktail.

"Ooh let's have sex on the beach that sounds nice!" exclaimed Megan.

"Albert!" shouted Billie. "We all want sex on the beach thanks!" Which made the three of them laugh hysterically.

Albert dutifully brought over the cocktails, "I thought that you would like some bread, hummus and olives with your drinks."

"Oh Albert I think I could marry you, this is so thoughtful of you" said Billie gratefully.

"This was complimentary with the drinks" said Albert modestly.

"Oh well we still love you." Said Billie.

"Gosh Billie you love everyone tonight, I don't feel special any more" said Megan jokingly.

"You know Meg, if I batted for the other side, there would be no one else but you, but I love men, so sorry mate" said Billie kissing Meg's cheek.

"I'll get over it!" laughed Megan.

"I have never had sex on a beach "announced Seren with a sigh.

"Oh I have "said Megan wistfully.

"Wow Megan you dark horse you." cried Billie.

"Yes well you do mad things on honeymoon, the tropical sun frees your spirit and you give way to the need to get naked and swim in the sea" sighed Megan. She can't remember when she last saw her naked body not alone anyone else.

"Gosh I can't imagine Patrick wanting to have sex on the beach" said Seren sadly.

"Since we have got married, I don't know it's all mortgages, carpets and paint. Our Friday nights are in B+Q not the Walk About any more. He is even talking about kids. I don't know I just want to get to know Patrick a bit, travel or I don't know have sex on the beach before being tied down with kids" groaned Seren in despair.

"Don't worry love it's over rated. Sand gets everywhere, I felt I was even peeing sand afterwards" laughed Megan feeling a bit better that she had been adventurous once.

"I would love to have a baby and settle down but I can't find a man!" said Billie.

Megan and Seren both looked shocked at Billie.

"You, you want to settle down. How long was your longest relationship?" asked Seren

"Mmm... 6 weeks?" Billie replied thinking.

"You don't give guys a chance. You are too busy trying to shag them and then you panic and run out of that bed before it gets cold." Said Seren. "No offence mate."

"I know" groaned Billie. "I do like the chase and get bored very easily, but a baby I just want one. My mum did alright bringing me up on my own."

"I know love but your mum didn't have a choice your dad died. It's hard you know, your mum was amazing bringing you up and I am sure you would be too. But don't give up yet, give the guys a chance hey. You are so stunning and strong, I know there is a guy out there if you gave him a chance" said Megan earnestly while holding Billies hands.

"Christ what happened to us, taking about this shit" said Billie pulling away. "Where is the drinks?"

"I need to go and powder ones nose, where does one go to do this?" Megan asked jokingly.

"I'll show you" offered Seren.

When Megan stumbled to the loo, she just about managed to flop onto the toilet seat as the cocktails had gone straight to her head.

Oh my god I've got to calm down, I can't drink any more. I should not have mentioned Billie's dad. She told herself. *Billie's dad had been a refugee from Somalia, Billies mum worked in the job centre and help him get a job had fallen in love with him, married him, and then the torture he had gone through got too much and he committed suicide. Billie's mum was left heart broken and pregnant. If only he knew it might have given him the strength to live? God Billies mother is amazing what the fuck am I complaining about*, she thought as she staggered out of the cubicle to wash her hands.

I have a family, a job and I don't look too bad. She reassured herself putting her fingers through her hair wishing she had brought her bag with her.

She took a deep breath, pushed the door open and walked out into the main hall determined to look sober as she could.

I'm fine she told herself *I can do this*.

She found Billie and Seren dancing to "Sex Bomb" and immediately joined in sexily gyrating hips to the music. As Megan twirled around in her dance, Billie grabbed her arm trying to speak but was laughing too much. Tears were flowing from her eyes as she struggled to breathe as she pointing downwards. Billie's screeching drew Seren's attention and when she saw that Megan had pulled up her comfy beige knickers over the skirt of her dress, showing the world and its neighbour her underwear, Seren burst into laughter too. Megan looked down to find to her horror what was amusing them so much. She screamed quickly pulled her dress down and sat down blushing covering her face with embarrassment.

"Ooh soft porn star next" said Seren as she summoned Albert over to order more cocktails. "Megan, are you ok hun?"

"Oh my god I feel so embarrassed" she said drinking the dregs of her drink.

"Oh don't, it was the best thing I've seen for ages love" said Billie starting to laugh again.

"Christ that was so funny" she screeched as Albert brought another three cocktails over to the table. Billie and Seren carried on laughing which soon made Megan's embarrassment dissipate and joined in the laughter, so much they were all gasping for air and eyes watered with pure joy.

"Oooh I fancy having a black Russian" mused Billie. Then eyeing up Albert as walked passed "Or white Russian would be even better" she suggested saucily.

"We'll have three black Russians please Albert" said Seren trying to be the responsible one. "Billie leave him alone now, love him, you're making him feel uncomfortable" admonished Seren.

"Ok mum" said Billie cheekily. "It's just there is something about his accent, he sounds like a villain in a James Bond movie."

"Talking about James Bond, isn't that Roger Moore coming over?" asked Seren through the haze of booze.

"More like Daniel Craig now Seren" whispered Billie in admiration.

Megan looked up and there stood the young blonde man who was staring at her when he was stood at the bar.

"May I ask this delightful lady in the red shoes for a dance?" he said in a crisp English accent.

"Of course you can" replied Billie quickly before Megan's had a chance to respond.

As Megan was trying to compute this incredible situation. She found herself being pushed in to this handsome stranger arms.

"Go then on Meg" egged on her drunken friends.

He smiled and guiding her to the dance floor and they slowly danced to George Michael's "Careless whisper"

Megan could hardly breathe, she was dancing in the arms of this drop dead gorgeous guy. He took his hand and gently pushed it into the small of Megan's back drawing her closer. The smell of his woody aftershave made her relax and she slowly managed to exhale as they danced cheek to cheek, which stopped her from fainting with desire. She felt his hips moving in sync with hers, then he skilfully guided her around the dance floor. Megan felt that he had some sort of magical power which made her feel as if she could actually dance as they glided around the dance floor. Every movement felt was so natural and sexually charged. God this was amazing!

Then to her horror the unfamiliar concoction of alcohol she had consumed suddenly began to make her feel nauseous so forcing her run off the dance floor leaving him confused and stranded on the dance floor.

Megan, in complete headless chicken panic mode somehow found herself in the kitchen and luckily found a bucket of tea towels which she uncontrollably vomited in.

Albert looked at her in disgust "Mu'dak! Why do you western women drink so much!" he exclaimed.

Megan's eyes stung with tears at the abhorrence of this reality. Alcohol had never made her sick before. She looked up and was horrified to see Billie, Seren. Even worse that the beautiful blonde vision had also witnessed the whole thing.

"You all right hun?" asked Seren gently.

Megan felt so ashamed, all she could manage was a mumbled apology to the watching ensemble and ran back over the dance floor, grabbing her bag and ran outside.

She stood on the step and breathed in the cool air trying to compose herself, feeling her burning cheeks ease in the chill night air. She could not help but noticed the beautiful reflection of the moonlit sky in the river that ran in front of the hotel. Megan thought *in another time or another dimension this would have been a wonderful romantic setting*.

Then from behind she heard a voice ask politely,

"Would you like some water?" She turned to find the

blonde Adonis from the bar offering out a glass of water.

"Yes please "Megan replied shyly taking the glass.

While sipping the water she noticed Billie and Seren peering around the doorway smiling and waving her on in encouragement.

Megan blushed and looked into this vision's grey eyes.

"Would you care for some air?" he asked.

"Yes" she said breathlessly.

Why on earth would he want to talk to me! I've just thrown up in front of him for Christ sake, she puzzled.

"I'm so sorry for …" Megan began.

"No problem, we have all been there" he said and offered her a handkerchief and pointed to his lip. "You have a little something" as she still had some vomit perched there.

"Oh god, how revolting am I?" asked Megan full of self-loathing quickly wiping her mouth with his handkerchief. "Thanks" she said offering it back. "Oh that's alright you can keep it and by the way you are not revolting, quite the contrary actually" said the blonde dream boat.

Then he surprisingly took her in his arms and kissed her fully on the mouth. Although Megan enjoyed the kiss she couldn't help but think how revolting he was kissing her after she had just thrown up.

I know I wouldn't kiss me now she thought to herself bemused.

"Hang on a minute!" said Megan snapping back to reality and pushing him away. "Is this a dare or a joke?" she asked accusingly quickly looking around expecting to find a bunch of giggling men.

"No" he said stunned at the accusation.

"Then why are you kissing me?" she demanded.

"Well, I saw an attractive lady with red shoes on and thought she might like to be kissed" he said as a matter of fact.

Oh my god my mother was right! Thought Megan. *He thinks I have no knickers*!

"I have got knickers on you know" she shouted.

"I know, I saw" he said smiling "shall we start again?"

"Ok" said Megan blushing.

It had been a long time since she had blushed before today and now she couldn't stop herself.

"Wait here" he instructed and turned and ran back into the hotel.

Megan stood there unable to move full of intrigue and

excitement about what this charming young man was going to do next.

Then he reappeared with a bottle of prosecco and two martini glasses.

"Where did you get them from?" Megan asked in surprise.

"I acquired them from the kitchen, I don't think anyone will notice as they are too busy shouting about somebody who has been sick in a bucket of tea towels! Yuk fancy that!" he said smiling.

"Oh how disgusting!" Megan said weekly laughing back "Can you imagine?"

"Hello my name is Max, would you walk with me?" he asked, "my hands are full so I am quite harmless" he added.

"Oh I don't believe that for a second but yes I will walk with you" Megan replied smiling.

They walked slowly towards the river where there was a picnic bench overlooking the romantic picturesque scene.

"I would offer you my handkerchief to sit on but I found that I am at a loss for one, sorry" he apologised.

"Don't you carry a spare?" Megan replied sarcastically.

"A lack of foresight on my part, Akela would never forgive me for, I am sure" Max said laughing.

"You were a boy scout!" exclaimed Megan.

"Well, a cub scout actually "stated Max.

Megan sat on the bench, "I feel so much safer now"

"Drat that was not my intention" said Max suggestively pouring two glasses of prosecco. "Haven't you ever heard the old adage, never trust an Englishman with sparkling wine?"

"No, I've only heard the one that says that it's ok to lose to anyone in rugby, as long as we beat the English." Said Megan laughing.

"Ooh that's below the belt" he said passing her the wine.

"Yes I know" said Megan smiling as she sipped the wine smugly.

Megan you are flirting she admonished herself. *God I forgot how much fun it was,* sighed and looked away.

"Isn't it beautiful here" she said recovering.

"Yes I didn't know how beautiful Wales was" said Max sitting next to her looking at the moon.

"Where do you come from?" asked Megan.

"Oh now I don't think you want to know that really. I am here as a visitor to your delightful country, let's not get bogged down with reality."

Wow thought Megan *a dream come true. A beautiful stranger no questions asked. Oh no should I be here? She thought as her* conscience kicked in. She drained her glass then poured another, *Fuck off Jiminy Cricket I'm having fun here*!

Max smiled and topped up his glass too.

"Well if we are to not to discuss reality, I am the rich movie star Fifi la belle" Megan announced.

"Oh yes I thought I recognised you, I am a spy of course" Max whispered.

"I thought so" agreed Megan.

"Ah, obviously not a very good one though" he said laughing. "If my cover was blown that easily."

"Well I am not really Fifi la belle but none other than Mata Hari" said Megan dramatically.

"Of course, only Mata Hari would realise that I was actually Max Bond" he said leaning over looking into Megan's eyes sending tingles down her spine.

Don't question it Meg enjoy it use the force, she envisaged *Alec* Guinness in her head. *God hark at me I must be pissed!* Thought Megan.

With that Max put down his glass, leant over and kissed her fully on the mouth again placing his hands in her hair. Megan instantly melted with desperate desire he had somehow created inside her. She dropped her glass wrapping her arms around him to kiss him back passionately. She felt her body being charged with electricity waking up her pelvic muscles like the ancient mummy in "Carry on Screaming" yes Max was jump starting her choked up passion. Oh my god the electricity was so intoxicating that she had to break away from the kiss for air then drank his wine.

"Wow you are breath-taking Mata Hari" said Max breathlessly.

The passionate kiss had ignited the pent up frustrations that she never knew she had kept inside her. Megan suddenly felt recklessly alive and immortal. So she stood up and she impulsively ran towards the moonlit river while removing her dress. At the river's edge she stopped and removed her boring beige underwear and in her brazen nakedness she reached out her arms letting the moonlight envelope her, curves and shape of her body.

Max looked on in amazement totally bewitched by this wild beautiful half shadowed figure before him. In the moonlight her alabaster skin looked so soft and smooth, he yearned to touch her skin, kiss her skin, lick her did she taste as wonderful as she looked. He conjured in his imagination of holding on to her soft rounded hips as thrusted his hard penis inside her. The shadow enhanced her ample bosom making her nipples appear so hard and erect, he found yearning to suck them, to taste her, to drink her. He was entranced by her ghostly beauty.

"God you're fucking fantastic!" He shouted.

This outburst made Megan feel so sexy and wild!

She shouted at the moon "I am Megan Cassagrande!" and recklessly jumped into the silver moonlit river.

She was soon followed by a naked Max shouting out "You are one fucking mad woman!"

The cold water sobered up Megan instantaneously "God its fucking freezing!"

"Yes it is fucking freezing!" said Max. "Come here and let me warm you up."

Of course, not wanting to be responsible for him getting pneumonia Megan swam over to him.

He looked at her wantonly, pushed the hair out of her eyes, kissing her passionately. She could feel his toned body up against her soft voluptuous body. Before she knew it their tongues were frantically exploring each other's mouths as they treaded water, holding onto each other tightly. She could feel his hard erection rubbing between her legs searching for her. Her body yearned to have him inside her as she put her fingers through his hair.

I remember Paul having hair, she thought dreamily.

Then her bloody conscience woke up! *What about Paul you love him don't you?*

You're married, you have children for Christ sake. I know I do but he's probably doing this in London himself anyway she reasoned to herself.

You don't know that, her conscience screamed as tears streamed down her face. She realised she could not do this and broke away from this hotly desirable young man because she knew he was just a fantasy and that in fact she loved Paul with all her heart.

"Are you ok?" asked Max concerned.

"I am so sorry. I can't do this. I am married you see, I've got a family" said Megan suddenly feeling like a small and pathetic creature. The spell was broken, she was back to being Mrs Jones.

"Oh "said Max stunned. " Not separated or divorced then wanting a fling?" He questioned hopefully

"No very much married I'm afraid and I love him too, I really do" said Megan realising at that moment how much she wanted Paul.

"Right" said Max realising that was the end of the fun and frolics tonight. "Better be getting back then" he managed to say and started swimming back wondering what had just happened.

Megan slowly followed him to the shore, feeling deeply ashamed and shocked by her behaviour. She quickly got out of the water and tried to dry herself using her large comfortable pants as a towel. She struggled to pull her dress down over her damp body and jammed her wet feet into her red shoes which seemed to be mocking her now. She picked up her support bra and tried to dry her hair in the ample cups, eventually she gave up and angrily stuffed her underwear in her clutch bag.

"I am so sorry "she said through her dripping wet hair "I am a stupid old woman"

"Hey" said Max looking effortlessly sexy as his shirt clung to his wet well defined body, "you are a very sexy woman and I enjoyed tonight, thank you." He said pushing the hair out of her face and Megan instantly melted with his touch.

Gentleman as ever, he took his jacket and chivalrously wrapped his jacket around her as she shivered. "Don't worry we have all got our problems, my fiancé shagged my best mate so I that's why I came to Wales to forget."

"Oh god, I'm so sorry" Megan said sadly as they walked back towards the hotel. "You needed to find somebody who would have shagged you, apparently revenge sex is the greatest and I have wasted your time."

"No Mata Hari, this is the most fun I have had almost having sex for a long time." Max laughed. "I think this encounter has done us both good."

"Well I don't know, it sounds a bit too Freudian for me."

"Hey I think this far too purvey for even Freud to understand" replied Max smiling.

"Hi Megan, thank god we found you! Why are you both so wet?" asked Seren coming towards them.

"Oh didn't you see the rain?" asked Max in a serious tone.

This made both Megan and Max laugh as he put a comforting arm around her while they walked towards the hotel.

"Taxi's here" said Billie softly to Megan.

"Goodbye Max it's been surreal" said Megan returning his jacket.

"Yes surreal, you could call it that I suppose. Goodbye Megan I will always remember tonight" he replied and kissed Megan's cheek.

Then he swung his jacket nonchalantly over his shoulder and noisily squelched back to the hotel.

The girls climbed into the taxi.

As the taxi crossed the bridge over the river, Megan watched the hotel get slowly swallowed by the trees, while becoming a memory that would keep her warm for years to come.

"Well, spill the beans!" said Billie excitedly

"Come on Meg what happened?" coaxed Seren.

"Nothing!" she said "Absolutely nothing" and then promptly threw up in her clutch bag.

"Oi if you're going to be sick you can get out of my taxi!" shouted the driver.

"No it's all right, I'm ok now!" shouted Megan while Billie and Seren looked at her repulsed at this puke filled creature they had created and opened the window.

Megan put her head on the cold window and smiled, holding on to her clutch bag full of vomit. She was in love with Paul and felt so lucky to have found out now. She hoped it was not too late.

CHAPTER 4

AFTER THE PLEASURE NOW THE PAIN!

The next morning Megan was woken up roughly by an angry Paul.

 "What the hell happened to you last night?"

"Why?" groaned Megan squinting through a fog. Her head was pounding and opening her eyes only made it worse. Her mouth felt dry and disgusting like the bottom of a budgies cage.

"God you stink, you smell like a pond!" Paul exclaimed.

"Pond? Oh yes I went for a swim" she vaguely recalled while gingerly trying to lift her head off the pillow.

"You went for a swim! You went for a swim in a bloody pond!" Paul shouted in disbelief.

"No, no a river" mumbled Megan sitting up now then grabbed her bed clothes as she suddenly realised she was naked.

"In a river! What the fuck did you do last night? And what have you done to your hair?"

"Had it cut" said Megan touching her hair which made her wince with pain.

"Oh by the way I don't suppose you know anything about the handbag in the sink downstairs full of sick!"

"Oh yes, I was sick" Megan mumbled as she tried to piece together the events of last night like a giant jigsaw of memories.

"I came home from London this afternoon to surprise you and I what do I find? You and this house in a fucking mess! Megan what the hell's going on?" demanded Paul.

Megan slowly stood up and put on her dressing gown,

"What's the problem? All I've done is have a haircut, went out for a drink with some friends, had a swim in the river and then came home." Megan stated as if this was perfectly normal. "Now I'm going to get some paracetamol if you don't mind."

Megan stepped over her wet clothes, which were strewn all over the floor and staggered downstairs.

Paul followed picking up Megan's clothes and angrily threw them in the laundry basket.

Megan got the paracetamol and dispensed some cold water from the fridge into a tumbler. She desperately gulped down the pills with the water, spilling some of the cool liquid down her front and wiped her mouth with the back of her hand like a navy. "Ahh that's better!" she gasped.

"Megan?" questioned shocked Paul.

"What?" asked Megan.

"Nothing, I'm going for a swim, we can discuss this when you are sober!" shouted Paul. With that he picked up his kit bag and stormed out slamming the door behind him.

Megan just about managed to make herself toast and coffee. She sat down and curled herself up in a ball in the corner of the settee to eat her breakfast while watching ET repeated on the TV yet again. Once the paracetamols had kicked in and her stomach settled. She then had a hot shower to cleanse her soul just as well as her aching body.

Feeling refreshed she dressed in a chambray shirt, grey jogging bottoms and tied a scarf around her hair like a makeshift Alice band. The need to exorcise the shameful memory of the night compelled her to strip her bed and determinedly marched down to the washing machine. She roughly shoved the soiled linen in the machine to a boil wash with extra fabric conditioner in attempt to remove any evidence of the night before.

She then took the incriminating bag from the sink and with her stomach turning over with revulsion that such offensive substance could come from her, she wrapped it in a plastic bag. She tied it up tight and disposed of it in the rubbish bin outside. The price of losing her purse, brush, lipstick and comfy underwear was the atonement for dancing with the devil.

Megan had polished the house, made the bed with the fresh clean purified linen. She made Paul's favourite lamb stew as a sacrificial offering while anxiously waited for his return.

Megan's stomach tightened upon hearing Pauls car eventually pull into the drive. She nervously sat at the dining table wringing her hands and head bowed waiting for the penance that she felt would inevitably be required of her.

Paul entered the house dropping his kit bag angrily kicking it away. He walked steely eyed smelling of a mixture of chlorine and shower gel toward the miserable wretch that was Megan.

Paul's eyes seemed to soften with the welcoming smell of the lamb stew. He slowly and deliberately took two crystal wine glasses out of glass cabinet, placed them on the table and calmly filled them with red wine, politely offering one to Megan. She was weak with relief as she gratefully took the wine and thanked him, but mentally prepared herself for the required confession.

Paul sat opposite with wine in hand and took a sip of wine with a cold expression he prompted Megan to talk by saying "Well, this should be interesting..."

Megan hesitated and took a deep breath before replying, "I've been feeling a little lost and down since Lloyd left, so the girls from work decided to take me out for a treat."

Megan stopped to read Paul's expression but there was nothing, he just was sat silently listening.

"So I had my hair done" she explained as she removed her scarf and shook her hair for Paul to see.

"Then I bought some makeup, a dress and shoes."

"And don't forget the bag" added Paul accusingly.

"Oh yes and the bag" she said flushing with embarrassment her eyes stinging with guilty tears that she was determined not to release. She rubbed her nose with the back of her hand and sipped her wine and then continue her confession realising that Paul was not going to make this easy for her.

"Then they took me out for a drink, to The Glyndwr hotel of all places" Megan continued her weak defence.

"Nice" said Paul sarcastically.

Megan knew from his tone that his patience was already beginning to wear thin.

"Well we ended up drinking lots of cocktails and I suppose, as my mother always used to say, you should never mix the grape with grain and well….. Before I knew it I got really drunk." Megan babbled on.

"And…." Prompted Paul.

"Then I was sick, so I went outside, met this charming nice man and went for a swim with him in the river." Megan blurted out relieved that this sin was out there laid bare on the table. "But I didn't have sex with him!" she shouted out in desperation after hearing herself actually saying her confession outload.

"I suppose I should be grateful that you didn't sleep with him! Christ Megan what the fuck was you thinking!" shouted Paul.

"I wasn't thinking!" she said losing her strength causing the guilty tears spill down her cheeks. Submitting to awful realisation that she had no defence for her actions and resigned that she was completely at the mercy of Paul's wrath.

"I was a fireman for Christ sake! Don't you think women have thrown themselves at me over the years? But I tell you this Megan I have never, ever strayed." Paul spat out in fury. "You were my wife, tirelessly looking after our children, working so hard keeping us whole as a family and I admired you and never wanted to hurt you. Christ Megan, I felt blessed and very fortunate man to be married to you." He managed to say suddenly exhausted by the build-up of emotion.

"Why, why, didn't you ever tell me" cried Megan.

"I thought you knew, I was here wasn't I" gasped Paul putting his head in his hands.

Megan slumped back in her chair stunned that Paul was using the past tense. Silence hung in the air punctured only by the sound of Paul and Megan's breathing.

"What now?" asked Megan quietly.

"I don't know" replied Paul.

Megan sat nervously watching Paul for any sign of forgiveness as they both sat silently sipping their wine.

"Would you like some stew Paul?" asked Megan in desperation.

"No Megan, I am exhausted I'll go to bed and I think it's best if I sleep in Iestyn's room tonight" and with that he used the last of his energy to get up and make his way heavily upstairs.

Megan sat stunned as she watched him leave.

Oh my god! What have I done? Thought Megan at the sudden realisation of the pain she had inflicted on Paul.

Paul her husband, the father of her children. The man she was supposed to love with all her being. How could she have done this to him? Could the marriage the life they built together be over just like that?

CHAPTER 5

FREEDOM BREEDS CHAOS

After a fitful sleep Megan awoke the next morning in her thick cotton pyjamas which had brought her no comfort last night.

Sunday the day of rest, well there is no rest for the wicked! Megan reasoned. Feeling a sudden fright on recalling yet again her mother's warnings.

Never go to sleep on a fight she use to say, have I lost him mum? Megan asked the heavens in desperation.

Megan put on her slippers, dressing gown and made her way downstairs to find Paul naked on the settee eating a family tub of Cornish Cream ice-cream watching a rerun of "Carry on up the Khyber" laughing like a drain.

Megan looked stunned at this mad man before her.

"Morning Meg!" cried Paul.

"What on earth are you doing?" asked Megan in disbelief.

"I am sitting here naked eating ice cream cos *I can!*" exclaimed Paul.

"That, that imported Venetian couch cost four thousand pounds and you have your naked skid filled arse on it!" replied Megan slowly.

"Yes, and encase you've forgotten I helped pay for this overpriced shit that you insisted on buying, so I can do what I like on it" said Paul with glee.

"It's cream!" stated Megan.

"I know! Laughed Paul hysterically. "And it's fucking uncomfortable too, what a total waste of fucking money!"

Megan left the room in disgust and made her breakfast. She noticed that Paul had not made the coffee as he usually did, so she resigned herself to make do with instant.

"Would you like some coffee?" asked Megan poking her head around the door.

"No thanks" said Paul happily.

Megan shut the door tightly taking her breakfast and coffee to the dining table wondering who this guy she was living with was.

"God!" announced Paul returning to the kitchen to put the empty tub in the recycling bin. "You forget how funny those films are!" he announced as he stretched.

 Megan sat there in stunned admiration of how good he looked naked.

What was I thinking? I should have been skinny dipping with him! Megan admonished herself.

Then she flushed with the memory of the total abandonment she felt when she jumped into the river.

"I think I'll have a whiskey!" announced Paul shattering her memory.

"Don't you think it's a bit early? Aren't you going to get dressed today?" asked Megan annoyed.

"Umm no, I don't see why I should have to. I'm not going anywhere and it's only you here so, fuck it, I don't think I will get dressed" he said pouring a generous whiskey.

"How long Paul?" asked Megan "How long is this punishment going to go on for?"

"Punishment, Jesus Megan this is not about you, you self-centred bitch! This is about me. Me! Remember me the loyal husband! The good father!" he shouted "Well Megan I am free from any responsibility now! You have released me and I thank you" said Paul bowing theatrically and left the room slamming the door behind him.

Megan looked at the shut door in shock, had she driven her sensible strong Paul to madness?

After getting washed and dressed she spent the morning doing the ironing whilst singing along to the radio.

All of a sudden Paul burst into the room wearing his tatty tracksuit and t-shirt on that Megan's had begged him to throw away.

"I know, let's have sex!" exclaimed Paul.

"What now? I'm doing the ironing!" Megan replied taken aback.

"You would rather do the ironing than have sex with me?" asked Paul in surprise.

"It's not that, it's just this needs to be done." explained Megan flustered.

"Why?" asked Paul "Why does it need to be done?"

"Cos otherwise I'll be all behind" explained Megan.

"Oh I love your behind" said Paul grabbing Megan's curved bum in both hands.

"Paul!" shrieked Megan smacking his hands away "What are you doing?"

"Being spontaneous!"

"Well can you be spontaneous later on?"

"That wouldn't be spontaneous then!"

"Look, I couldn't relax anyway as I would know the ironing hadn't been done. It's alright for you to say, hey let's have sex, but come Monday morning when you have no shirt ironed you will soon moan."

"Christ what happened to us that making love has become such a chore" said Paul sadly walking away.

Megan stood frozen to the spot with iron in hand.

What did happen to us?

Megan then carried on to finish the ironing, it was as if she was hardwired to do it. In the words of Magnus Magnusson, *I've started so I'll finish* controlled Megan. Then she heard the front door slam.

There were tears in her eyes as Megan inspected the t shirt she had just ironed. She was suddenly gripped by panic. *What if that's it? After twenty five years, over in an instant, just like that.*

When you haven't got a clue what to do, just carry on, doing what needs to be done reasoned Megan.

She unplugged the iron and laboriously put the clothes away

The phone rang and she pounced on it hoping it was Paul.

"Hi mum" said Lloyd.

"Hi Love, how are you?" replied Megan trying not to sound disappointed at the sound of her son's voice.

"I'm great thanks."

"How are you getting on with everyone?"

"It's ok, because I can cooks so I'm not short of friends."

"Oh good, good" Megan smiled towards heaven, *Thank god you taught him how to cook mum.*

"How is the course going?"

"Ok so far thanks. I just thought as its Sunday and you would be cooking lunch about now so I would catch you in" said Lloyd sadly.

Megan looked around at her empty cold kitchen and sighed.

"Yes I'm making the Sunday roast love, for me and your dad."

*"Miss you both "*Lloyd whispered.

"I miss you too love" Megan replied with tears in her eyes.

"Well I had better ring off now mum as I have lots to do" said Lloyd suddenly *loud* and cheery.

"Yes of course, thanks for ringing love bye" Megan replied.

"Bye speak to you soon" and he was gone.

Megan felt so lost that she decided to ring Angharad.

"Yeah Mum" said Angharad hoarsely and coughing.

"Are you ok?" asked Megan concerned.

"Yeah, I'm ok, went out for few drinks last night and you just woke me up" said Angharad yawning.

"Oh sorry love, just wanted to know if you were alright" Megan asked unsure.

"Oh I'm brilliant thanks mum!" said Angharad more enthusiastically.

"What time is it?" Came a man's voice in the background.

"I don't know "whispered Angharad laughing.

"You got friends over?" asked Megan.

"No only Brock's here" said Angharad.

"Morning Mrs Jones "called Brock's deep Canadian voice.

"Morning Brock" shouted Megan back.

"Oh he's gone to the bathroom sorry. Like I said, heavy night last night mum. Everything ok with you?"

"Yes, yes fine I'll get back to making lunch then I just wanted to check you are ok?" said Megan putting on a cheery voice.

"Oh Sunday dinner, mmm, I'm jealous, I really miss them mum. Bye the way have you heard from Lloydie?"

"Yes he is fine, settling in well or so he says"

"Oh good, hey Brock you will have to try my mums Sunday dinner one day." Shouted Angharad across her room.

"Yes it'll be great to meet him" said Megan.

"Got to go now, mum thanks for ringing give my love to dad, bye."

"Bye" said Megan but Angharad had already gone.

There was no point in ringing Iestyn as his Sunday lunches were very popular. Iestyn only rang when he needed something so no call from Iestyn means he was fine, so all the family are ok.

By the timed Paul had returned later that night Megan had put all the ironing away and vigorously cleaned the house, while a chicken roasted in the oven.

"Hungry Paul?" asked Megan in desperation.

Buoyed by her children's enthusiasm of her Sunday dinners and as Megan's mum had always drummed into her that the way to a man's heart was through his stomach, providing a cooked dinner seemed a good start to make up with Paul

"No thanks "slurred Paul "I'm off to bed."

He staggered up the stairs went into Iestyn's room and deliberately and loudly closed the door.

Megan felt Paul had put a dagger in her heart by refusing her offer of food yet again. She angrily turned off the oven wrapped the cooked chicken in tinfoil and put it in the fridge then went to bed herself, saddened by the how much Paul seemed to want to hurt her.

She lay in bed feeling the great wall between her and Paul and didn't know what to do to bring it down. She touched the bedroom wall behind her wondered if he was awake, thinking about her like she was thinking about him. She wanted to run into Iestyn's room beg for forgiveness and make mad passionate love to him but the fear of his rejection was so deep that she couldn't move. She was paralysed with indecision so did nothing except lay there with her eyes open in the large cold bed, wishing for the sun to come up.

It'll be better in the morning, she told herself.

Megan had somehow managed to fall sleep as she was rudely woken by the alarm, dazed she looked at it, she realised she was laying across the both side of the bed hugging Paul's pillow and her heart sunk when she realised she was on her own.

She tiptoed over to Iestyn's bedroom and furtively opened the door. She was disappointed to find that Paul had already gone. The bed empty and neatly made, only his clothes neatly hung over a chair. Feeling exhausted and helpless Megan resignedly got herself ready for work.

When you haven't got a clue what to do, just carry on doing what needs to be done, this was turning into my mantra now sighed Megan.

CHAPTER 6

THE SUBSTITUTE

Back in work Seren sidled up to Megan putting her arm around her and asked "Hey honey why you are so down?"

"Oh Seren, I've messed up big time with Paul, I told him what happened Friday night and now he can't even look at me" sobbed Megan. "Do you think he'll want a divorce? Oh my god, my kids will come from a broken home!"

"Has Paul left you then?" asked Seren trying to understand what Megan was telling her.

"No... not yet" replied Megan cautiously.

"Well don't you think that's a good sign and that he still wants to be with you?" asked Seren gently passing her a tissue.

Megan wiped her eyes and smiled "Do you think?"

"But nothing happened with "The man from Atlantis", did it?" probed Seren.

"No... nothing" said Megan defiantly.

"Well then, you just need to talk to each other. You both obviously love one another may be you just need to remind each why."

"Thanks Seren, I hope your right." said Megan pulling herself together.

Then there was a knock at the door.

"Come in" Megan called out, then to her surprise she found "the man from Atlantis" standing in front of her.

"Oh are you Mrs Jones?" asked Max unsure, in a smart brown Jacket, open neck white, dark trousers and highly polished brown shoes. He looked even more attractive in the daylight and looking irresistibly lost.

"Yes I am and what you are doing here?" demanded Megan in disbelief, quickly removing her spectacles.

"I'm the substitute teacher covering for maternity leave" replied Max smiling at Megan's discomfort. "I have been instructed to report to a Mrs Jones, or should I call you Mata Hari"

"No, Mrs Jones will suffice thank you" replied Megan replacing her glasses and adjusting her cardigan in an attempt to regain her professional composure.

"Well, Mr Craig wasn't it?" Interjected Seren smiling trying to diffuse the tension. "Shall I escort you to Jaynes Classroom?"

"Mr Abraham, Max Abraham" he said in a bondesque way.

Megan swooned, *God even his name is gorgeous* she thought exchanging a helpless look with Seren.

"Just follow me then, Mr Abraham" said Seren mimed to Megan a gasp of approval.

71

With an arch of his eyebrow, he smiled knowingly at Megan, as he followed Seren.

"We are so glad you have arrived. We thought Jayne would be having her baby in the class!" giggled Seren shyly as she could not help be affected by his stunning good looks.

"Jayne, please meet Mr Abraham, he's come to cover your maternity leave." announced Seren, as she entered the classroom.

"Oh thank god!" exclaimed Jayne with so much relief she fell back in her chair.

"Are you ok?" asked Max rushing forward concerned.

"I am now you're here" said Jayne who seemed to be oblivious to his good looks. "You are a welcome sight I must say."

"Well, I 'm glad I've made someone's day" laughed Max.

"I'll leave you both to it then" said Seren as the school bell rang summoning the children to line up outside on the playground

"Thank you miss…" enquired Max.

"Seren, Mrs Seren Young" said Seren smiling and left saying "Good luck Mr Abraham. Glad to have you aboard."

It unsettled Megan knowing that Max was in the building with the potential of repeatedly bumping into him, to remind her how sinful she was. She tried to bury herself in her work but she couldn't get Max out of her head.

Beautiful Max, gorgeous Max. What was she doing? She berated herself. I am trying to get my husband back not bonk the substitute teacher.

Mr Evans then entered Megan's office, "I would just like to say Megan I like what you have done with your hair?"

God that's all I need to wake up Mr Evan's testosterones. Why did I start all this? Why wasn't I happy with my lot, why did I have to change? Megan moaned to herself I despair.

"Thank you Mr Evans and how your wife is?" asked Megan pointedly.

"Oh, she's going away for the weekend" replied Mr Evans smirking.

Oh god no screamed Megan in her head then abruptly changing the subject said "A Mr Abraham has arrived to cover Jayne's maternity leave." she announced as professionally as she could.

"Oh right, where is he?" asked Mr Evans back in work mode.

 "He is in the classroom with Jayne" replied Megan.

"Gosh he must be keen, better go and speak to him." said Mr Evans as he left Megan's office.

Thank god he's gone thought Megan putting her head in her hands and breathed out.

Why me? She gestured towards the heavens.

The phone rang "Hello "Megan demanded.

"Meg it's me" said Paul in unsure voice. "I have to go to London tonight for a few days, maybe this is for the best? Put a bit of distance between us eh?"

"Yes" said Megan feebly but in her head she was saying, *no don't go, lets sort this mess up.*

"I thought so, I'll let you know when I'm on my way back." Then the line went dead.

Megan sat down at her desk exhausted and cried.

At break time Billie came in to Megan's office, "Have you seen... have you seen him!" said Billie excitedly.

"Yes, I have seen him" Megan replied resignedly.

"Oh Megan are you ok?" asked Billie concerned. "I just thought it was funny that somebody you err…. swam with," the word swam being punctuated with hand gesturing quotation marks, "Happens to turn up here of all places."

 "I know and Paul's so angry with me too" said Megan pacing her office. "And there is no need to do this "mimicking her punctuation mime.

 "I did only swim with him and nothing else and now bloody Paul has gone to London to work."

What, how does Paul know?" asked Billie in surprise.

"Well I told him I got drunk and went swimming with someone but he doesn't know he is here now in all his gorgeousness" she replied and she slumped back in her chair defeated with exhaustion.

"Oh Megan, but you love Paul don't you? So if Prince Charming tries anything on, just kick him into touch and focus on Paul….simple." Said Billie.

In came Seren slamming the door, "Oh my god he is gor…geous!" she exclaimed. "And you…."

"Nothing happened" Megan shouted "We just bloody swam!"

"Ok, ok "said Billie pulling Seren away from Megan protectively. "We believe you." Then nudging Seren to prompt her to add, "Yes of course nothing happened."

"Right, now we have got that sorted" said Billie taking control. "What should Megan do?"

"Nothing" said Seren.

"Nothing?" asked Megan.

 "Yes Megan you can't do anything until Paul is back. Just be polite to Max, keep him at arm's length. This will give us time to help you think of a way to patch things up with Paul" Seren replied using her teacher tone.

"Ok Mrs Young." Chorused Billie and Megan.

"Come on Billie let's have a coffee before the bell goes, I need it" demanded Seren and both Billie and Seren left Megan's office.

There was a gentle tap on the door.

"Come in "shouted Megan as she tried to file some records.

"Hi" said Max. "Jayne made you a coffee."

"Thank you" said Megan taking the offered mug of hot coffee trying not to look at him.

"Are you ok? I just wanted to apologise for my behaviour Friday" said Max gallantly.

"Your behaviour, no I should be sorry, not you" insisted Megan looking at his earnest blue eyes which took her breath away.

"No I shouldn't have let you jump in the river. I shouldn't have taken advantage of you, you were drunk" he said sorrowfully.

"But you didn't take advantage of me" replied Megan sounding regretful as she said it.

"Oh thank god for that so we can be friends then" exclaimed Max.

"What?" asked Megan abruptly woken up from her fantasy.

"Well they do say never get your honey where you make your money."

"You're telling me not to shit on my own doorstep" shouted Megan.

"Or you could say that" replied Max.

"Get out Max!" shouted Megan.

"I am sorry if I have said something wrong" said Max holding the door.

"No Max you said the right thing. Thanks for bringing me back to my senses." said Megan, while smoothing down her ruffled feathers as he left.

Now I must not get distracted. I've got to concentrate on getting Paul back.

But how?

CHAPTER 7

ROMANCE IN THE AIR?

On Saturday morning excited as Paul telephoned the night before to let her know he was coming home today. She jumped out of bed, hurriedly got dressed in the jeans and t-shirt she had worn the evening before, and then headed for Marks and Sparks. Megan decided she was going to get a meal deal for two and sit down to talk with Paul over a glass of wine.

She took a basket and walked determinedly around the store picking out steak, veg, profiteroles and of course wine. She just became aware of something dragging on her foot when Mr Evans came in her view.

"Megan "he called out "Fancy meeting you here!"

"Oh, Hello Mr Evans" replied Megan whilst shaking her leg trying to discreetly shake off what was on her foot. Upon looking down at her foot, to her utmost horror she saw the offending article were in fact her pants from yesterday!

"Oh come now Megan we're not in school now, you can call me Ken. As Amy has gone to her sisters last night. I thought I would just picking up a curry for one, Amy hates curry" he whispered in a conspiring manner.

"Oh nice "replied Megan automatically, not really paying any attention to the conversation, instead she was desperately trying to secretly untangled her foot from her old pants without drawing attention to her embarrassing predicament.

"Are you busy tonight Megan?" asked Mr Evans encroaching in on Megan's personal space.

Just at that moment Megan successfully flicked her pants free and watched aghast as they flew across the floor but fortuitously disappear under the fridge. Relieved she cried out "Yes thank god!" as she grabbed Mr Evan's arm to steady herself.

"Pardon?" asked Mr Evans confused.

"Yes I am busy sorry Mr Evans" she said quickly letting go of his arm. "In fact I'm having a romantic meal with my husband tonight" announced Megan a bit too loudly. "I'm so excited about my husband arriving back from London" She babbled on unable to stop talking. "Ooh it's like our honeymoon all over again every time he comes back." *What am I saying?*

"Oh that reminds me, I need to get champagne!" she continued.

"Oh yes of course champagne" mumbled Mr Evans dejectedly.

"Have a great night with your curry" said Megan mockingly, while filled with immense pride at managing Mr Evans and yesterday's knickers all in one go.

Oooh and I could get strawberries as well thought Megan.

Megan had paid for her goods she made her way upstairs to the lingerie department bought some sexy red underwear and left happily for home. She smiled to herself imagining what the staff of Marks and Sparks would think when they found an old pair of used knickers abandoned in the food dept.

Once home she had a luxurious Jasmin bubble bath, shaved her legs and moisturised. She excitedly popped on her new underwear and dressed in a red blouse, fresh jeans and finished the look by applying some make up. Megan looked at her reflection satisfied that she looked smart but sexy.

She then waited eagerly for Paul to return home.

As time passed her carefree attitude had been replaced by desperation. On his eventual arrival Megan jumped up and hugged Paul so hard he had a job to breathe.

"Megan let me go "he gasped.

"Oh I am so sorry, I am just so pleased to see you." Megan said as she released him.

"Why no swimming trips while I was away?" asked Paul sarcastically.

"No "said Megan sweetly, trying to ignore the dig. "No swimming darling, champagne?"

"Champagne!" said Paul astounded "What have we got to celebrate?"

"We are celebrating getting to know each other again!" announced Megan.

"Ok….. I'll drink to that?" said Paul hesitantly. "Just let me get in first." he said taking off his coat and putting his bag down.

Megan ran back to the fridge excitedly and took out the champagne. She had never opened a bottle before, but in her head she was now going to be a sophisticated lady and started to untwist the wire.

"Well I must say this is nice surprise" he commented as he walked into the kitchen noticing the candlelit table with soft music playing.

Suddenly then the cork popped out of the champagne bottle and hit Paul square on the forehead knocking him clean off his feet while the champagne frothed spilled over the floor.

"Oh my god! Are you ok?" asked Megan kneeling down by his side the bottle still in hand frothing everywhere.

"Yes, yes I think so!" said Paul dazed and tried to get up.

Megan noticed that Paul had a red mark in the middle of his forehead and started to laugh.

"Charming I must say, first you try and strangle me then you knock me out!" said Paul sitting up against the kitchen cupboard.

"Oh Paul" said Megan laughing while passing him the bottle to hold by now they were both covered in champagne. Megan lowered herself to the floor opposite him and her back against the kitchen island. Paul took the chilled bottle held it against his forehead to soothe the pain then took a big swig from it.

"How much have you drunk?" he asked passing the bottle back.

 "Believe it or not nothing!" she gasped then took a big swig herself, making the bottle fizz again and flow up her nose making her choke.

"Gosh Meg, you still can't drink from a bottle!" exclaimed Paul grabbing the bottle back he laughed out loud "You mad woman!"

They passed the champagne bottle back and forth taking it in turns to drink from it and every now and then Paul would put it against his bruised forehead for relief.

"I'm sorry I wanted this to be so romantic," said Megan apologetically. Looking at them both sitting on the floor covered in champagne.

"Oh I don't know, this could be romantic" said Paul suggestively.

"Well you look like you have a love bite in the middle for your forehead" laughed Megan.

"What?" said Paul getting up and looked at himself concerned in the mirror. "Oh my god Meg how long will that last?"

"God knows" said Megan laughing, drinking the champagne and trying to stand up on the slippery floor which made Paul laugh too.

"Perhaps I should put the steak on your head?" suggested Megan as she reached for the fridge.

"No don't waste a good steak! That's funny they never suggested that you carry around a lump of steak with you on any first aid courses I've attended" laughed Paul.

Megan eventually composed herself enough to cook the meal and they both sat at the table.

"God how time flies, I remember a dashing young fireman being a guest at our school fete, showing the children his fire engine" Megan reminisced as they ate there meal.

"Do you know, I really hated going to those things, all those snot ridden kids climbing all over our highly polished fire engine. Then low and behold a there was a parting of the waves of horrible demanding children and an Aphrodite appeared" said Paul with his blue eyes looking at hers.

"Oh and I thought you loved children" said Megan looking away to ease the sexual tension she was feeling and sipped her wine.

"Oh no Megan I hated the disgusting creatures but I was fascinated by the tanned, nymph that was before me with her stunning long dark ebony hair. I was mesmerised by the school's young new secretary, fresh from university I was told.

Megan blushed and sipped her wine as her mouth had gone dry.

Paul laughed "I can't believe that I can still make you blush Meg! After all these years. I can't remember when I saw you blush last."

"It's probably the wine" dismissed Megan.

"I was tanned as I used to spend summers in Portugal with my "Avo", my dad's mum" said Megan, as her eyes filled with memories of summers long gone.

"Megan I do love you" said Paul seeing Megan retreating back inside herself.

"I love you too" said Megan, as she stood to clear the plates. "I got profiteroles for desert."

"Leave the plates Meg" Paul said earnestly reaching out his hand to touch her arm.

"I can't "she whispered Megan as his touch suddenly filled her with anxiety again.

*What the hells is wrong with me? S*he thought as she took the dishes to the sink.

She turned around and Paul was gone.

CHAPTER 8

HALLOWEEN

Megan stood in a flowing long powder blue organza dress, on a bow of a ship. She watched Monaco which was slowly disappearing in the sunset as she sipped her cocktail cuddling with Paul, who was looking tanned and handsome in his tux.

"Oh Megan, how I love you" he said as he slowly leaned over to kiss her.

Then the phone rang and woke her up with a start from her blissful dream.

Fuck who could be ringing me on a Saturday morning? Bastards!" groaned Megan.

As she came to her senses, she suddenly realised she was all alone in bed so she picked up the phone.

"Hello" she answered politely as she could.

"Hi Meg," it was Billie.

"What do you want?" groaned Megan disappointed.

"Oh sorry if I woke you. I've been up hours already and had a swim before I began my marking."

"Well done, I 'm pleased for you" said Megan sarcastically as she struggled to sit up in bed.

"Oh dear, somebody's got out of the wrong side of the bed this morning."

"Actually I'm still in bed. Was there a reason you called?"

"Oh yes, The Manor is having a week of scary Halloween evenings, it's the last night tonight and Seren's got us some tickets. "

Oh bollocks! Thought Megan but thankfully "Ok" came out of her mouth.

Didn't they know she hated Halloween, she never understood the concept of being scared witless in the name of fun.

"What does it entail?" she asked cautiously.

"Oh you go around the Manor while they re-in act some of the old legends of the house, or something. The Morgan's ancestors were pirates after all, so it should be good fun and it's had great reviews" encouraged Billie.

"How scary is it?" asked Megan asked hoping not to seem too wimpy.

 "Well everyone is saying it's scary but it says on the ticket you only have to be over eight to go, so it can't be that bad can it?"

"Ok could be good I suppose" said Megan looking around her empty, cold immaculate bedroom.

"You ok Hun?" asked Billie concerned.

"Oh… yes, I 'm fine thanks…. just missing Paul I suppose."

"This will be perfect then for you then mate. Pick you up at eight" she rung off before Megan had chance to say anything.

Ok what does one wear to be scared shitless? Thought Megan opening her wardrobe. *Brown trousers' perhaps* she giggled to herself.

Eight O clock came and Billie was at the door dressed in jeans, boots and bomber jacket. Megan was relieved as she had opted to wear jeans too. She had hoped it wasn't going to be a dressy affair even though they were off to a Manor.

"Ready" said Billie excitedly.

"Yes I suppose" said Megan grabbing her bag and Jacket. "Ready as I'll ever be."

As Megan got into Billie's blue VW Golf she noticed Seren and Max already seated in the back.

"Oh, Hi Max, what a surprise, I didn't know you were coming." Megan said glaring at Billie and Seren.

"Oh didn't I mention Max was coming, Oh how lax of me. Oh well, we are all here now, no biggy" said Billie looking ahead avoiding eye contact with Megan and feigning concentrating on driving.

"I think I have been kidnapped" said Max.

"Oh what a drama queen, you love it really" said Seren pushing him back in the seat.

"Well we are here now" sang Billie.

She parked the car and they walked to the grand entrance to the Manor.

"I am so sorry Max, You do know I had nothing to do with this don't you" apologised Megan.

"Don't worry I know" replied Max annoyed.

While Seren showed the tickets at the reception Megan noticed a person dressed as a vampire playing a piano.

Oh this is not going to be that bad thought Megan with great relief.

"Good evening everybody" addressed an elderly pale gentleman dressed in a smart black suit to the group. The group consisted of about ten adults and five children. "I am Grayson, Lord Morgan's butler. It is 1671 and he has come back from Jamaica to settle back in his homeland of South Wales. It is my pleasure to guide you all through the dark and gruesome history of the House."

Billie smiled and squeezed Megan's hand as they followed Grayson with the rest of the group to a highly ornate dining room.

Grayson guided the group to stand around a long grand dining table set for a banquet. The lights suddenly went off and there was the sound of thunder in the air. On the dining table appeared a glass bowl lit up with a dismembered green woman's head with black curly long hair. It's started to tell the group of the time Rob "Blackbeard" Morgan invited his affluent enemies to a grand banquet and how he got his revenge by poisoning them all.

I can cope with this. Megan told herself. *It's a woman dressed up under the table.*

Megan turned to remark to Billie how clever it was when she found herself was face to face with the Grim Reaper holding a lamp in one hand and a scythe in the other. Megan screamed in fright. She then noticed there were more grim reapers surrounding the room which in turn made the children begin to scream. The grim reapers blew out their lamps and disappeared, then the lights came on.

"Are you alright?" said Max who was now standing next to Megan.

"Yes "said Megan shaken but embarrassed as the adults glared at Megan as they calmed their children down.

"She'll be fine" said Billie cheerfully.

"It was a very clever effect, I'm very impressed" Seren joined in.

"Ladies, Gentleman and of course the delicious….. I mean delightful children" announced Grayson. "We have lots more to see, through here please."

He held open a door to a dark corridor, the group entered hesitantly in single file. Megan looked into the dark corridor and instinctively reached out to hold a hand which happened to be Max's hand. Max held firmly onto Megan's hand and winked reassuringly. Megan smiled and entered the dark corridor with Max behind her. In the darkness

Megan felt cobwebs brush over her face and felt some small objects fall over them. Megan closed her eyes and followed the group silently gripping onto Max's hand to the sound of children squealing in excited delight.

The corridor led to a large room which at the one end had a lady laden with jewels and grandly dressed laying on a table with a man dressed in an Elizabethan costume standing over her.

"I am Lord Morgan" He shouted. "This is Isabella the love of my life who has betrayed me."

With that he pulled out a dagger and cut the woman's throat.

Megan held her hands to her face and froze in horror as the lady lay there with blood gushing from her neck.

Grayson then shouted "Run! Run quick the door as he's going to kill you!"

Megan turned around in fright and could not locate the door they entered by, but noticed a very small door at the far end of the room. Megan's flight or fight instinct kicked in. She ran with tears in her eyes and a voice bellowing "Get out, Get out, run for your lives" ringing in her ears towards the very small door. Possessed by shear fright she selfishly pushed the screaming children out of the way and made her way through the door. Feeling safer in a grand well-lit landing she breathlessly waited at the bottom of the staircase for the rest of her group. When Billie and Seren managed to leave the room they ran towards her.

"Are you ok? Oh my god Megan your face was a picture," they laughed.

Max came to her side and softly asked "Are you alright? You don't seem to be handling this well."

"I know I'm terrified, my brain just won't let me except it's all make believe. I am so sorry "said Megan visibly shaking with tears welling up in her eyes.

Then BANG! There was a blood curdling scream as a dummy of woman dropped down from above and hung by a rope around her neck. The dummies feet were right by Megan's head. Megan screamed even louder and buried her head in to the back of Max's jacket. Max struggled to breathe as Megan had pulled his jacket up around his throat.

Max helplessly mouthed "Help" to Billie and Seren.

Between them both they quickly managed to prise Megan off Max to enable him to breath. Max recovered and took charge, he gave Megan a hanky and said to Billie "Look I'll get Megan out of here. You and Seren carry on and we'll meet in the Stonehouse Pub by the car park."

"Ok "said a shocked Billie taking Seren's hand to follow the group. The parents looked relieved that Megan wouldn't be able to terrify their children anymore.

Max then asked the alarmed Butler if there was a way he could get Megan out.

"Oh no you can't go back its just one way, as the next group is coming behind" said the butler in a matter of fact voice.

"Isn't there any way I can get my friend out? Look at the state she's in." implored Max.

The butler looked at the pathetic creature before him and took pity on her. He unhooking his radio from under his jacket and made a call.

"Charlie come to the ground floor emergency exit please and bring a lantern" he said in a calm warm welsh accent.

Then few minutes later a man appeared dressed in black and wearing a balaclava deliberately rolled up to show his face, holding a lantern.

"Charlie can you escort this lady and gentleman off the premises place. Waving your lantern in front of you as we previously discussed."

"Oh yes, just in case it got too much for the kids" said Charlie looking surprised at the tear stained full grown adult woman in front of him.

"Err... yes well can you just escort them off the premises so I get in with the rest of the entertainment."

"Yes of course, come on both, follow me" said Charlie.

Charlie opened the fire exit and escorted them through a maze waving his lantern as they walked. Now and again men dressed in black popped their heads out asking Charlie if all was well.

"Yes just someone too scared to cope with any more surprises" replied Charlie.

"Oh cool man we must be doing a good job then" cried a young voice.

"Yes get ready we will soon be out here so get back to your places" instructed Charlie.

"Here you are both, the carpark. The tour is over so will you be ok from here?"

"Yes thanks "said Max handing a tenner over to Charlie. "Thanks again."

"Yeah no bother mate thanks "he said smirking and ran off into the darkness.

Megan relieved, gave Max a big hug.

"Thank you" She cried and before she knew it she kissed him full on the mouth.

She then recoiled in horror, "Oh I am so sorry Max. I was so relieved to get out of there"

"Hey that's ok, damsels in distress are compelled to do that, it's a normal reaction" laughed Max. "Come on let's get you a drink. "

Megan followed him into the pub and sat at a table by the open fire while he got her a brandy to settle her nerves.

"I am so sorry about tonight, I didn't know I was going to be so terrified. I hope I haven't spoilt your evening" said Megan as she knocked back her brandy.

"No problem, this wasn't my cup of tea either. People prancing about in costumes trying to scare people well ….." Max stopped himself so as not to hurt Megan's feelings any more. "I'll get you another drink, perhaps a longer one this time."

"Thanks I'm feeling a lot better for that. Yes a gin and tonic would be great" replied Megan blushing.

Max came back with two gin and tonics.

"I am so sorry I have never behaved like that before it's as if the children leaving home have taken my strength with them, I have never felt so weak and feeble."

"Are things better with your husband now?"

"Oh Paul, fine, fine thanks. How is your love life going?"

"Oh not bad, I've been kissed twice by a beautiful woman both in very strange circumstances" said Max "so one can live in hope."

"I'm sorry Max but there is no hope with me I'm afraid but thank you for saying I was beautiful" smiled Megan glowing in the warmth of the compliment.

Then in rushed Billie and Seren, "Well fuck me that was bloody brilliant!" shouted Billie with excitement.

"What happened?" asked Megan.

"Oh I am so glad you weren't with us Meg, you would have had a bloody heart attack!" exclaimed Billie.

"I'll get us some drinks "said Seren, letting Billie regale her story.

"When we got outside we were chased by a man in a hockey mask with a bloody chain saw no less" exclaimed Billie. "Well I nearly shit myself, it was fantastic!"

Seren came back with the drinks and continued…. "Well I must say the funniest thing tonight was seeing Megan push those young kids out of the way to be first out of that room. Well done, Roger Bannister couldn't have done it any faster" announced Seren.

"Here's to Megan" cried Billie. "Here's to Megan. Who we now know will never save us from a ghost!"

They all cheered and laughed, as they carried on drinking, a goodnight was had by all.

CHAPTER 9

BREAKFAST IN BED

Sunday again! Megan groaned to herself as she clutched her aching head, as she struggled to sit up in bed amongst all her cushions which she had uncharacteristically failed to put in the ottoman last night.

God I have got to stop this. I have never drunk so much.

She turned on the radio to listen to the Sunday morning love songs which she usually enjoyed but instead this morning the words in the songs seemed to taunt and annoy her.

That's what's wrong with me. My head is full of romance and roses, a fantasy that doesn't exist. It's just something that films, books and songs have made up for us….. It's all a big fat lie! She said to herself as she threw one of her precious satin cushions at the wall.

Then there was a tap on the door then Paul popped his head around it.

"Morning Meg" he said cheerfully.

He then pushed the door open to reveal a tray with a cafetiere, choc au pain and a red rose.

"Breakfast!" Paul announced with pride.

"Oh my! How lovely" Megan managed to cry out in complete surprise and joy.

Paul walked in dressed casually and placed the tray on Megan's lap.

"Well I got to thinking about the old house in Portugal and how you loved choc au pain for breakfast when we stayed there and so I popped out to the 24hr supermarket and low and behold they had freshly baked choc au pain."

"It was meant to be" said Megan with tears of guilty gratitude in her eyes.

"May I join you?" asked Paul politely.

"Of course "agreed Megan and held on to the tray tightly as Paul sat next to her in bed.

"We haven't been to Portugal for years" said Paul as he poured the coffee.

"No we haven't said Megan smelling the rose. "I got too upset when they built that holiday complex by Avo's House."

"We should see if any work needs doing to it?" Paul suggested. "You father would not like it to go to wrack and ruin.

"Mam was so upset when dad died, she never wanted to go there again." Megan shrugged.

"There are some good memories there too love" coaxed Paul.

"I know" said Megan sipping her coffee. "These choc au pain are lush."

Paul realised the discussion was closed.

"At least there is something I do right" said Paul smiling.

"I'm sorry for being so distant" replied Megan.

"I'm here waiting for you to come back to me. I know you will come back to me" said Paul gently. "You do realise I have always been in fourth place, sometimes fifth."

"Oh I'm sorry, have I been that awful?" asked Megan sorrowfully.

"No, I wouldn't have you any other way Meg, you are so caring" cooed Paul and then looking in his blue eyes Megan just crumbled and kissed him passionately almost upsetting the coffee. Paul quickly grabbed the tray to save the day.

"Close shave! "He exclaimed.

"Quick reactions Mr!" said Megan in admiration. "I can remember you coming to the school in your uniform with some safety leaflets for the children. God you made my head spin I can tell you Fire Fighter Jones."

"Well that's why I did it, I knew that women were suckers for men in uniform" said Paul laughing.

"So you didn't have to come back with the leaflets?" asked Megan.

"No of course not, I just got all dressed up to impress you and it worked" said Paul smugly.

"I don't believe you!" cried out Megan.

"You agreed to go out with me didn't you?"

"I know, how I could resist this tall dark stranger so smartly dressed in front of me."

"What about now Megan could you resist me now, a few follicles lighter with a few extra pounds?"

"Oh Paul I love you so much" and leant over to kiss him again "But I'm trapped by this tray" laughed Megan.

Paul laughed, "This coffee is going to go everywhere. Perhaps we should finish breakfast first otherwise you'll be moaning that I have ruined your duvet."

Ever the practical Paul thought Megan disappointed, *he didn't throw the tray away and take her roughly now. Although Megan reluctantly realised that Paul was right in that she would have moaned if the duvet cover had got stained. She had obviously knocked the confidence out of Paul over the years and she suddenly felt ashamed.*

They sat closely eating their breakfast together. Megan couldn't remember the last time she had been so close to Paul. She felt so happy and contented being close to Paul listening to the radio.

"Paul I haven't been happy and I don't think you have too" said Megan bravely.

"Is that why you went swimming in a river do you want somebody else. Don't you love me anymore Meg?" asked Paul, his big blue eyes filled with fear.

99

"No Paul I do love you, I just want excitement, I want to feel young, and I'm always so tired and drained. I want to be

exciting Megan Cassagrande not boring Mrs Jones. I want to feel interesting, pretty, I just want to feel again. I want an affair perhaps but with you. Paul is it possible to have an affair with your husband?"

 "An affair you say?" pondered Paul he then took away the tray and nervously he asked "Megan can I tell you something."

Megan felt her heart stop in fright, as she answered "Of course, what is it?"

"Well, for a start I hate your bloody pyjamas! I feel like they are a barrier to keep me away. They are so thick, I can't feel you anymore when you sleep next to me. It seems as if you are deliberately you barricading yourself away from me" said Paul seeming relieved that he manage to say it. He sat in front of Megan looking anxiously in her eyes waiting for her response.

Megan was in shock, *after having Lloyd had she shut him out? Lloyd had been such a rough birth.*

 She looked back in to Paul's eyes remembering him saying that he would never let Megan go through that again. Looking at Paul she realised he was back there too.

"I nearly lost the both of you Meg that day" he managed to say.

"Oh god, Paul why didn't you ever tell me" Megan said with tears rolling down her cheeks. "I will take them off now."

With that Megan took off her thick warm comfy pyjamas and hid under the covers.

"I want you to be comfortable Meg" said Paul softly.

"I know "said Megan squirming under the covers. "It's just well …. I was a few dress sizes smaller and a few less stretch marks in tow."

"Megan you are so beautiful, now more than ever" said Paul softly.

He leant over and kissed Megan deeply, his probing tongue finding Megan's yearning mouth, which made her pelvic muscles spasm. This feeling evoking distant memories of the way she use to feel on just catching the sight of Paul when they were young. His well-toned body, his thick dark hair and his wicked take me to bed smile.

"I know "said Paul.

He picked up the tray left the room and returned with a bottle of wine and two glasses.

"Oh brilliant so now you need to be drunk to make a pass at me" said Megan annoyed and frustrated.

"No just to relax you Meg, if we were having an affair, wouldn't you think wine would be involved, wouldn't you think it romantic." said Paul softly ignoring Megan's scowl.

"It's a bit early isn't it?" asked Megan as she took the glass.

"Too early for what?" coaxed Paul "It's just us here being sinful."

She smiled and drank her wine, leant back against the headboard and closed her eyes to let Nat King Cole's voice and the wine intoxicate her so easing her tight muscles. Paul drank his wine watching his wife's face relax to reveal the

smiling beautiful carefree girl that cast a spell over him at the school fete all those years ago. He revelled in the glow of the sight of her again.

Megan went to take a sip of wine and found the glass was empty. She opened one eye and saw Paul staring at her. She felt her body tingle under his gaze.

"What are you doing?" Megan accused.

"Can't a man admire his beautiful wife?" questioned Paul gently.

"Well it's a bit strange isn't it?" said Megan sitting up again.

"Here have mine" said Paul and exchanged her glass for his.

Then he lit the candles that Megan would never allow to be lit. Megan tensed knowing how much she had spent on those candles but wisely said nothing just sipped her wine quietly wondering what was her husband going to do next?

He went into the ensuite and picked up the almond oil he had left there earlier.

"Does Madame requires a massage" suggested Paul in a French accent.

"Oh Paul it's been years…." Said Megan smiling brightly.

"Shh" said Paul putting his finger to her mouth. "I know I am sorry for neglecting you for so long."

Megan finished off what was left of Paul's wine in one gulp placed the glass on the bedside cabinet then obediently turned over and laid on her front in submission.

Paul smiled and removed the duvet in one stroke to reveal Megan naked, which made her gasp. Then Paul boldly straddled her, taking the cap off he rubbed it into his hands to warm it up. He then began to firmly massage Megan's' shoulders. It felt good touching her smooth soft warm skin again, it was an amazing turn on to feel her body relaxing to his touch and her soft moans.

"Ooh Megan your muscles are so knotted, you are so tense" he said as Megan softly moaned "Yeah I know "as she felt the knots dissipate through her body. She could feel his erection move on her back as he worked harder on her shoulders which sent tingles through her body. He then moved his hands down her spine which made Megan groan involuntarily, Paul struggling to control his great desire gently kiss her shoulders.

Megan could feel his erection on her back growing.

Then just as Paul began gently licking her spine, the phone rang.

"Shit! " Paul cried out so violently it made Megan recoil and tense again.

"Yes" he answered the phone abruptly.

Megan felt her face go crimson with embarrassment and made a dive for the duvet to cover her now cold naked body.

"Oh no, don't worry I'll be right there now, no worries. Don't cry I'll come and get you and bring you home." Paul voice had changed from rage to concern in an instant. "I'll be right there."

He put the phone down shouted "That fucking Brock!"

"What happened?" asked Megan concerned.

"Angharad came home to find Brock shagging her flat mate Kim" stated Paul angrily.

"Oh no poor love" said Megan in despair. "I'll get dressed. "

"Thank Christ I didn't drink much wine" cried Paul. "Bastard!"

Megan and Paul quickly got dressed. Megan put on a blue top, jeans and then added a white scarf with delicate blue butterflies print.

"What the fuck Meg" screamed Paul.

"What?" she replied putting on her blue pumps, as she followed Paul.

"The scarf!" screamed Paul getting in the car.

"It goes with the top" explained Megan as she jumped into the car.

"Christ" shouted Paul as they sped off to rescue Angharad.

His head full of visons of their beautiful perfect little girl who had ruthlessly had her heart ripped out by a bloody Canadian swine.

Paul went speeding down the lane to find to his horror that his hands couldn't grip on the steering wheel of his speeding car as his they were so slippery from the oil.

"Fuck!" screamed Paul as he fought to grip the steering wheel to prevent his car smashing into any oncoming traffic on this narrowing lane.

"What?" replied Megan alarmed.

"I can't grip on the steering wheel!" He shouted in despair.

"Oh let me take it!" yelled Megan but the steering wheel was slippery and she made the car veer to the right over the other side of the road.

"Get your hands off the fucking steering wheel Meg!" screamed Paul trying to gain some control over the car.

"Alright no need for that I was only trying to help!" screamed Megan. "It was your idea to use oil remember!"

"That's right it's my fault to want to have sex with my fucking wife!" screamed Paul as he desperately tried to steer the car back to the left to avoid an oncoming car.

"Paul there is no need to take that tone!" shouted Megan. "You men, you are all the same, just like animals wanting sex all the time."

"No you don't Megan" shouted Paul. "You are not blaming me for this!"

As he managed to pull over and stop at a bus stop and breathed out in relief.

"Blame you for what" said Megan not letting up.

"For Angharad's boyfriend shagging Kim" shouted Paul as he got out slamming the car door. He started rubbing his hands down his jeans.

Megan sheepishly got out of the car, "I am sorry."

"Megan I'm not the bad guy here, you are the one that's fucked up! Yes you the perfect Mrs Megan Jones did something wrong without a thought for me or the kids" Paul shouted while rubbing his hands in his t-shirt.

"Sorry Paul here have my scarf" said Megan.

"Thanks, there is some bloody use for this after all" he said as he went back to the car and rubbed the steering wheel with it.

Which made Megan smile.

"Look love I have had twenty years of don't touch me, or not now I've got a head ache, the kids will hear. Look Meg I am usually the one that doesn't paint the walls quick enough, smooth enough, is that the colour I chose. I am usually your fucking pariah. Now you want me to be fucking Casanova. You just take the fucking biscuit you do!"

Megan stood frozen with shock at the outburst of anger that Paul had felt towards her all this time. She had been oblivious to the way she had pushed him away.

"Come on Meg, Angharad needs us!" Paul shouted from the car.

Megan hurriedly pulled herself together and got in.

"I'm sorry "mumbled Megan feeling totally at a loss.

Paul was on a roll now his frustrations flowing out of him at his captive audience who for once was stunned into silence.

"Do you remember when I use to cook you tea and run you a bath cos you were finishing work late Meg? How many times you came home exhausted and rejected my cooking and the bath. You never even said thank you, you just announced you were too tired and went to bed. There is only so much a man can take so I stopped bothering because you stopped bothering Meg."

"I didn't realise" said Megan feebly with tears trickling down her cheeks. She opened the glove compartment to find some tissues. "I just wanted the kids to be ok. I wanted to do my job as best as I could and give you all a home, a home you would be proud of. Is it too late for us?" said Megan blowing her nose it the serviette she found.

"Only if you want it to be" said Paul looking ahead at the traffic. "Anyway we have Angharad to sort out now."

Megan sat in silence until they pulled up outside Angharad's college digs. She had pulled herself together and pushed Paul to the back of her mind as she had done for years and composed herself to knock on the door.

Angharad opened the door revealing her unkempt strawberry blonde hair with red eyes, tear stained face and runny nose. Megan gave Angharad in big hug while listened to her daughter go over the pain and hurt this thoughtless Brock had caused. When Angharad had finished Megan gently guided her to the back of the car. Paul then loaded Angharad's bag into the boot.

"Got your keys love" whispered Paul to which Angharad nodded as she blew her nose in the big wad of tissues she had in her hand.

Paul then shut the front door, got back in the car and drove his wife and little girl back to the safety and security of home.

CHAPTER 10

A WELCOME DISTRACTION

Paul and Megan were both grateful for the distraction of having Angharad back home as it meant they could avoid talking about their faltering relationship. They just focused on Angharad. They provided tissues and a shoulder to cry on and of course loads of chocolate. Paul had come back to the marital bed, *probably for Angharad's sake* thought Megan. Megan didn't know the new rules, so was too scared for her body to stray into the forbidden territory of Paul's side of the bed.

Paul manged to escape the drama after only one day, as he conveniently had to go to Manchester. Megan felt relieved as she couldn't relax or sleep with him in the bed. Megan found the mouldy forgotten strawberries in the fridge and sighed remembering how excited she was to buy them and sadly threw them out.

After a few days Megan gently convinced Angharad to get showered and dressed. The shower worked its magic in making Angharad feel like she had re-joined the human race. The confidence to reach out and ring her old good friend Amy. Who responded by inviting her over to re-tell the awful tale to fresh sympathetic ears.

After work Megan asked Billie, Seren and Jayne who was bored on her maternity leave to an emergency drink in the Crows Tavern.

"So what's occurring Meg?" asked Billie straight to the point.

Megan took a big gulp of wine and said "Well I have just found out that I have been pushing Paul away for years. What can I do to pull him back?"

"Oh wow, you did have a weird weekend!" commented Jayne as she drunk her orange juice.

"Oh god don't look now "whispered Megan horrified. "Max is by the bar."

Megan had been trying hard to avoid Max but he kept on making her coffee every break time and just seemed so chatty.

"I know" said Jayne looking guilty. "He is such a sweetie and he doesn't know anybody here so I just had to ask him along, you never know he could help"

"Help?" exclaimed Megan in disbelief.

Max had bought a pint and was looking towards them. Jayne struggled to stand up and waved her hand. "Over here Max!"

Max smiled and walked over in all his gorgeousness and said "Good evening ladies, would you mind if I join you?"

"No of course not" said Jayne giving Megan a warning look. "Come and sit by me."

Jayne's hormones had obviously brought out her mothering instinct, thought Megan.

"How you managing going solo with my class?" asked Jayne.

"Ok thanks, they are a great bunch. How's your maternity leave going?" replied Max.

"Exhausting, I'm on a cleaning frenzy so when Megan called for this emergency meeting I thought Hallelujah!" exclaimed Jayne.

"What's wrong, why do you need help? Is there anything I can do?" asked Max sincerely.

Megan ignored Jaynes, "I told you so look" coughed and embarrassedly said "Well I need to get my husband back."

"Oh my god he hasn't left you because of the other night?" asked Max shocked.

"No" refuted Megan pointedly.

Megan felt her feathers ruffle and the girls excitedly moved forward into a huddle in for the gossip.

"No "Megan continued "I told my husband we went for a swim and he was fine with that."

"Never!" said Billie surprised," then why are we here?"

"Then what's the problem hun?" asked Seren gently touching Megan's' hand.

Megan took another gulp of wine, "Apparently I've been pushing Paul away with the kids work etc. and I want him

111

back. But I am lost and I haven't got a bloody clue how it?" she said with relief that she had managed to tell them.

"I'll get you another drink" mumbled Max uncomfortably, "anyone else?"

This relieved the tension then they huddled together to think about Megan's problem.

"When is Paul back from Manchester?" asked Jayne taking the helm.

"Friday, I have to pick him up from the train station at eight pm."

"Right" said Billie, "This calls for prosecco and strawberries, I think."

"Oh I have just thrown out strawberries!" exclaimed Megan. "Well they were mouldy, I suppose."

Max returned with a tray of drinks and asked "So how far have we got, formulated an action plan yet?"

"Unfortunately not" said Megan sadly "Anyway, Angharad's home now so maybe I should be concentrating on her instead."

"Oh god Meg she is young, she'll bounce back" reassured Seren.

"I know I'll ask Angharad and Amy over mine for a girl's night on Friday" suggested Billie. "It'll give you both some space" added Billie conspiringly nudging Megan with a wink.

"You sure?" asked Megan.

"Of course not, it'll be fun!" exclaimed Billie enthusiastically. "I'll get some Lambrusco in, we can put on some chick flicks, make voodoo dolls of ex-boyfriends, we'll have fantastic time."

"Oh no don't you think they are better off drinking jagerbombs and getting laid Meg" Max sarcastically suggested.

"So much for Mr Sensitive" said Megan annoyed.

"I'm just repeating what someone once told me that there is nothing better than revenge sex" said Max looking casually but seriously at Megan who went crimson with the memory.

Seren noticing Megan's discomfort jumped in suggesting "So pick him up from the train station looking absolutely stunning, then get him home give him prosecco and strawberries."

Max scoffed and put his beer down. "Why do women always have to complicate things? Why don't you pick up Paul from the station in nothing but a mac and high heeled shoes? Then just casually drop it into the conversation that you are naked under your mac and I can guarantee he'll have such a hard on that when you get home, if he waits that long, he'll be so desperate he'll just bend you over the kitchen table, job done." He said sitting back and drunk his beer in smug celebration.

"What!" said Megan in disgust, but really feeling turned on by the thought of it so much so if Max pushed her over this table there and then and had his way with her she wouldn't complain.

"God isn't it hot in here!" said Megan fanning herself with a tablemat looking for around for a window, for the fresh air she suddenly required.

"Oh my god that's fucking fantastic!" said Billie laughing hysterically and clapping.

"You look so cute and wholesome and then you come out with something like that!" said Jayne looking shocked." I don't think that our Meg could manage that "added Jayne looking concerned at Seren.

"Just stick with the prosecco and strawberries" suggested Seren kindly.

"Ok, just to set the record straight nice guys can be driven to wild passion by the right woman" said Max.

The gauntlet had been thrown Megan thought in her wine filled mind.

"He also hates my pyjamas" cried out Megan as the second glass had kicked in.

"What's wrong with your pyjamas hun?" asked Seren.

"I think this calls for another drink" said Billie getting some notes from her purse and giving it to Max, "would you mind getting another round in please?"

"Glad to be of service" said Max relived to get a break from this conversation.

Which made all the girls sigh and coo at how nice he was.

"What did he say about your pyjamas?" asked Jayne kindly.

"He hates them, he said they were a barrier between us and I'm not sexy in them. But what can I do, I can't wear nothing? I don't want him to see everything do I?" said Megan in despair with tears in her eyes.

"Oh hun don't sweat so love, this is easy to put right. Go to Marks and Sparks and get some negligees" suggested Seren.

"Negligees?" questioned Megan confused.

"Nighties" explained Billie.

"Oh I don't know" said Megan unsure.

"Oh come on Meg, it's a no brainer "said Seren. "They cover up the bits you don't want to show and they create easy access for the bits he wants."

This made everyone laugh hysterically.

Max returned to the table with the drinks asking "What's the joke?"

Which made them all laugh again, they thanked Max and grabbed their drinks.

"A toast "announced Billie. "To Megan."

"To Megan" they cheered and clinked glasses.

"And all who sail in her" added Max cheekily which made everyone laugh again. Even Megan after hitting him on the arm had to laugh.

After drinks were finished, Jayne suggested she drove everyone home.

"Hey Max where are you staying?" asked Jayne, as they all got in her black Mondeo.

"Over at Mrs Prices B&B" said Max.

"Oh careful with her she'll tell everyone your business mind."

"Her bloody cat drives me up the wall" moaned Max. "Princess for Christ sake!"

"I know "said Billie. "Why don't you come and stay at mine. I have a spare room and the money would be nice."

"Thanks if you're sure?"

"Course, also I wouldn't gossip about you love. I'm very discrete."

"Thanks Billie that would be great" said Max.

Megan felt a twinge of jealously.

What am I doing, I am trying to get Paul back she told herself, *Max can do whatever he likes, it's of no consequence to me.*

"Why don't you bring ring your stuff over Saturday?" suggested Billie as they pulled up outside her house.

"Ok thanks will take you up on that offer then" said Max gratefully.

One by one Jayne dropped everyone off until they reached Megan's.

"You alright hun?" asked Jayne.

"Yes, thanks. It was good night, I'm glad I got everyone together" Megan replied suddenly feeling tired.

"You're alright with Billie honing in on Max?"

"Of course, I love Paul. Billie can do what she likes, with the likes of Max Abraham" said Megan determinedly.

"That's ok then, good night" said Jayne giving Megan a goodbye kiss on the cheek.

"Thanks love, you had better be getting home before you have this baby in the car" said Megan laughing.

"No chance, it's too lazy by half that's why I think it's going to be a boy" said Jayne laughing and drove off.

Megan waved her friend off and put her key in the door, thinking how lucky she was to have such good friends. The combination of the company and the alcohol had her left with a pleasant inner glow, as she walked into her empty house, she felt warm, happy and content and not so lonely any more.

CHAPTER 11

SHIT OR BUST!

Seren and Megan were a little quieter in work the next day nursing soreheads, while Billie annoyingly still looked sparkling and bubbly.

Probably due to her new lodger, thought Megan. *Now, now Meg none of that please,* she chastised herself.

At break time, Max brought Megan a coffee which seemed to be becoming a habit now.

"Thanks Max, though I thought you would be making Billie coffee now" said Megan slyly.

"No she's going be my landlady that means her out of bounds" said Max casually sipping his coffee. "Why, would you mind?"

"No of course not. You can do what you want Max Abraham" said Megan *a bit too fiercely* she thought guiltily to herself.

"I know I was only joking, I know that Paul is the only one for you. You liked my suggestion of meeting him in your mac and nothing else though didn't you? I could see it in your eyes" said Max smiling wickedly.

"As if I would" huffed Megan, "none of your silliness here please."

"You can act all coy to the others but I know the Mati Hari inside of you." Max conspired. "I think Paul would like her too."

"You don't know my Paul" accused Megan.

"Well he is a man isn't he?" he said knowingly as he left her office.

Megan shook her head "What would he know?"

Then smiled wickedly to herself, "Could I...?"

Friday came around quickly and Seren wished Megan best of luck for her appointment in the beauty spa "Aphrodite." As Megan crept in the Spa she was greeted by a very sparkly enthusiastic blonde receptionist wearing a mint green tunic and black trousers.

"Good Afternoon, Mrs Jones is it?"

"Yes, but please call me Megan"

"Hi my name is Jane, I believe you are booked in with Hannah today, for a strip wax. "

"Yes" Megan managed to say as she blushed.

"If you would like to follow me Megan, I'll show you to Hannah's consultation room. Would you like a glass of water?" Jane asked as she guided Megan into an aromatic room which contained two chairs and a massage table.

"Please would you remove your clothes and pop this dressing gown on as Hannah will joined to" with that she left the room.

Megan did as she was instructed and sat on the chair Jane offered and waited nervously for the beautician to arrive.

By now Megan's mouth was dry and stomach began churning.

Perhaps she should have had the glass of water that was offered.

Just before she could chicken out and make a run for it, Hannah arrived.

"Hello Mrs Jones, it's lovely to see you again, your looking very well" said dark haired Hannah wearing pink tunic shaking Megan's hand.

"Hello?" asked Megan quizzically.

"Oh I am sorry I thought you would have remembered me? I'm Hannah, Mr Evan's the headmaster's daughter. I used to go St Anne's" explained Hannah.

"Oh my god, Hannah! Yes of course, gosh haven't you grown!" exclaimed Megan.

"Yes, this is my business now, I've just taken it over and it's really well thankfully."

"Well done" said Megan in shock.

"You still at St Anne's?" asked Hannah.

"Yes I am"

"I can't imagine St Anne's without you!" continued Hannah. "So you are booked for a full leg wax and a Brazilian."

"Well if you are too busy, it's not urgent" said Megan trying to discreetly move off the chair towards her clothes.

"No that's fine, you're booked in."

"Oh ok "said Megan as she reluctantly sat on the massage table.

Hannah tilted the table up so Megan was sat upright.

"Have you had this done before Mrs Jones?"

"No and please call me Megan"

"Oh ok Megan, gosh it's so weird calling you Megan."

"Yes" said Megan through gritted teeth.

As Hannah spread warm wax on Megan's leg "Don't worry this won't hurt much" she said laughing.

"Mmm that does seem nice" said Megan in surprise.

Rip "There you are first strip "announced Hannah cheerfully.

"Umm" said Megan gripping on the table and biting on her lip.

Rip "See it's not that bad!"

"Uhhu" said Megan with tears in her eyes.

"Right that's the legs done, now that wasn't so bad was it?" chirped Hannah as she moisturised Megan's legs.

"No" squeaked Megan.

"Right I'll just move the bed back down" said Hannah brightly.

Oh my god please let me be abducted by aliens, thought Megan as she laid back and closed her eyes. *Perhaps if I go into a trance I can forget I am here?"*

Hannah carried on chatting as she had her nose almost up Megan's vagina. "Yes Dad always speaks highly of you Megan, you were always so lovely to me in school….."

Oh my god can this get any worse? This is worse than having a smear!

Right this shouldn't hurt!" said Hannah as she *ripped* off the strip.

"Jesus fucking Christ! "Shouted Megan horrified as she watched the expression on Hannah's face turned to shock. "Oh my god, I am so sorry Hannah."

"No, don't worry" said Hannah trying to forget that her beloved school secretary could swear like a trooper. "That's fine, everyone has a different pain threshold. So just hold on, here we go again" and she quickly ripped off the strip again.

"Bastard! Bitch! Oh my god I am so sorry I really didn't mean it" explained Megan in horror as if she had just spoken in tongues.

"Well we do have a no tolerance policy of verbal abuse to staff but as I know you, we won't say any more about it" said Hannah quietly.

"Thank you, Thank you" said Megan shooting off the table and getting dressed as quickly as possible while trying to avoid any eye contact.

"I'll just leave you to get dressed, goodbye Mrs Jones, nice to see you again" she said politely and left.

Christ thank fuck that's over thought Megan in relief and wiped the tears of pain and embarrassment away in the dressing gown.

She paid her money quickly and left a big tip smiling at Jane while thanking her.

"I am pleased you had a good experience, hopefully we will see you again soon Megan" sang Jane brightly.

Over my dead body! Megan thought.

Megan rushed hot faced and sore to the sanctuary of Marks and Sparks. She visited the lingerie dept. and quickly grabbed a couple of negligees and some sexy underwear then guiltily went to the food section to buy prosecco and strawberries. Megan could hardly look at the spotty faced young lad at the checkout, as she put the underwear on the conveyor belt.

Where is a female assistant when you want one? She asked herself.

Then she wanted the ground to open up and swallow her as he held up a scanty negligee and shouted to a colleague "There is no price on this Ken, do you know how much they are?"

Red faced with embarrassment, Megan quickly paid the bill, grabbed her bag of transgressions and left the store as quickly as she could to the haven of her home. Breathlessly she rushed up to her bedroom and shut the door.

"Everything alright mam?" asked a concerned Angharad through the bedroom door.

"Yes I'm fine" said Megan while quickly taking off her coat and shoes. She left her bag on the bed, quickly composed herself and walked casually out of her room. "Fancy a cup of tea?" she asked.

"Oooh yes please Mam," said Angharad.

As they went down to the kitchen Angharad asked "How's your day bin?"

"Oh fine thanks, are you looking forward to tonight?" asked Megan while making the tea.

"Oh yes I am well chuffed that Billie asked me and Amy over, it's gonna be tidy."

"That's great that is love" said Megan relieved. As they sat on the stools at the kitchen island clutching their mugs of tea. "How are you feeling now?"

"Oh yer know mam, a day at a time" said Angharad.

"Yes love" said Megan feeling so proud of her little girl. It was almost Christmas break so she had a bit of time to heal.

"Found a new place to live yet love?" asked Megan.

"Yeah that was easy, Jenny, Nick and Brad have got a spare room since Ashton's given up his course and gone home"

"Nick and Brad?" Megan questioned accusingly.

"Oh god mam this is the twenty-first century, you know!

That's why Jenny wants a girl to move in to help back her up with all the guys. I'm not looking for anyone else, I've got to get over Brock mam." Angharad tried to reassure Megan.

"Ok sounds very sensible I must say" said Megan pleased.

"Well I do take after the best mam" said Angharad

"Oh thanks babe" said Megan and they both gave each other a big cwtch.

The doorbell rang "I'll get it, it's probably Amy" shouted Angharad as she ran to the door. Megan went to put the kettle back on smiling and feeling all warm from Angharad's cwtch. They were few a far between nowadays so she wanted to make the most of this proud glow she had.

"Hi Megan" said Amy dropping her backpack down and sat on a stool as Megan passed her a mug of tea. "Oh ta, you must be a mind reader, I'm spitting feathers, I am."

Megan smiled as the two just drank their tea and started to gossip and totally forgetting she was there.

It was good to see Angharad so animated and happy. Thank god that Amy had got a job in Matalan to save for college. All Angharad's friends were scattered around Britain in their chosen universities, doing their best on their courses they hoped will bring them a job to pay off their mounting debts. I didn't know how lucky my generation was, thought Megan.

The doorbell went again, Megan left to answer the door as the girls had not even drawn breath or had any recognition of the doorbell ringing.

"Hi Billie" said Megan smiling as she opened the door.

"Hi hun" said Billie giving her a big hug. "Ooh ready for tonight?" whispered Billie wickedly.

"As ready as I can be I suppose, the girls are through here" said Megan showing her to the kitchen.

"Ready then girls!" exclaimed Billie.

"I'll get my stuff!" said Angharad excitedly.

"Do you wanna cuppa?" asked Megan.

"No thanks tar" replied Billie sitting on one of the stools with her car keys in her hand. "I've not long had one thanks."

"I love your boots Billie" said Amy in awe.

Billie had black thigh high boots on with leggings and a baggy sweatshirt, she looked effortlessly stunning. "Oh thanks mate, got them in the sale last year."

"Ready!" exclaimed Angharad as she appeared with her backpack.

"Tidy then let's rock girls!" said Billie enthusiastically.

"Bye Mam" said Angharad as she gave Megan a kiss on the cheek.

"Bye Megan, thanks for the tea" said Amy as she darted after Angharad.

Megan walked to the door with Billie to see them all get into Billie's purple peugeot107.

"Have a good time" called out Megan as she waved them off.

"And you too" cried Billie winking as she drove off.

Megan sighed and turned to her empty house.

Ok it's now or never said Megan to herself.

CHAPTER 12

CASSEGRADE REVEALED!

Megan wished she could have a stiff drink for courage but as the whole point of this was that she was Paul's lift home, she knew this was an impossibility. She shaved and had a quick shower before she could chicken out. She blow dried her hair, scraping it back into a tight ponytail. She then put on her make-up, she was going for "Robert Palmer Addicted to love" look she thought to herself as she put on her bright red lipstick.

With a daring thrill she put on her beige mac over her naked body, slipped on her red shoes then liberally sprayed herself with Chanel No 5 to enhance the look.

Ok I'm Megan Cassagrande tonight she said to herself as she checked her reflection.

Shaking with nervous excitement she left her warm safe house. The breeze blowing up her coat making her feel incredibly naughty as her nipples hardened with the cold. She walked carefully in her heels, her heart racing, hoping that her neighbours would not see her. She sighed with relief when she sat in the safety of her car, turning on her radio to help her relax. She was thankful when the car started and she could make her way to the station. Cussing her shoes as her heels kept on catching her car mat but miraculously got to the station with time to spare.

Megan made her way into the foyer to see if the train was on time.

Megan positioned herself on the platform to make sure Paul could see her. Unfortunately as the train came into the station the sudden rush of air caused her coat to blow up around her head exposing to the world her freshly trimmed Brazilian including her shocked husband. Pushing down her mac in horror she saw that Paul was with his mate Mike who had been his best man at their wedding. With her face hot with utter embarrassment and tears in her eyes Megan lamely greeted Mike with a handshake, avoiding all eye contact.

"Hello Meg, I met Paul on the train and he kindly said you would give me a lift home." said Mike trying behave like nothing was wrong.

"That's fine of course, of course "mumbled Megan as she carefully walked back to her car desperately holding her coat down.

Paul and Megan couldn't look at one another in the car.

"I couldn't believe my eyes when I saw Paul on the train" said Mike busily talking to cover the awkward silence in the car.

"Yes that's nice" said Megan stiffly feeling as if she were dying inside.

After what seemed like an eternity Megan arrived at Mike's house.

"Thanks, do you want to come in for a drink?" asked Mike automatically. "No I don't think so" said Paul stiffly.

"Oh go on "said Megan choking back the tears. "Go on and have a drink with Mike, you can walk from home from here."

"Well if you would prefer me do that" said Paul confused.

"Yes, of course it would be good for you to both catch up."

"Ok then" said Paul "I'll see you later then."

Megan sped away and as soon as she got home she poured herself a stiff drink cried into the glass of whiskey. While she took off her makeup she pondered on the disastrous evening and what Paul would make of it.

Later that night Paul slipped into bed and cwtched into Megan's back "Thanks for the thought love." He whispered in her ear.

"Sorry it went tits up" said Megan sleepily.

"Well at least everybody didn't get to see them" laughed Paul.

With Megan having Paul cwtch into her back she felt warm, safe and happy.

"Night love"

"Night Meg"

CHAPTER 13

TRY, TRY AND TRY AGAIN!

Megan opened her eyes in the morning after having the best sleep she had for ages to find Paul's side of the bed empty. Megan got up with a start thinking she had dreamt his return last night.

Paul then appeared in the bedroom with tray holding prosecco, two flute glasses, chocolate sauce and the strawberries.

"Look what I found in the fridge. Let's have a picnic in bed!" suggested Paul.

"Why Mr Jones, what does that entail?" asked Megan excitedly.

"Well firstly I pour some prosecco for us" said Paul as he filled the glasses. "Then we dip the strawberries in the chocolate sauce and eat them accompanied with the prosecco."

"Oooh that sounds wonderful, but with an added condition that you must remove your clothes before you re-enter this bed" demanded Megan.

"Well I have warn you" said Paul taking off his top. "That I'm up a few dress sizes too." He added taking off his jogging bottoms and jumping into bed.

Megan squealed with excitement still clinging to the duvet "Oh Paul, you are so mad!"

"You drive me mad!" he growled and kissed. "Ooh, I like the sexy negligee."

Megan blushed as red as her satin nightie.

"I threw all my pyjamas away" Megan said shyly.

"Why Mrs Jones that is music to my ears!"

They both toasted "To us," drank the prosecco and ate the strawberries dipped in chocolate.

"God this is heaven" exclaimed Megan relaxing as the prosecco started to work its magic. She then giggled as she accidently dripped chocolate on her one breast which had somehow escaped the confines of her nightie.

"May I?" asked Paul politely.

His soft polite tones felt like velvet brushing over Megan.

"Feel free" she replied breathlessly feeling the excitement building within her.

Paul gently moved forward and with the gentlest touch his cold tongue from the chilled prosecco licked the chocolate off Megan's breast. Megan closed her eyes as she felt the sparks from his touch awaken deep desires buried within her. She felt young, pretty and desirable with her strong fireman again. Paul took another strawberry deliberately dropped the chocolate on Megan's the sort warm flesh of her tummy. This made Megan giggle, causing her to take a deep intake of breath and eagerly waiting for his next move.

"Whoops" he said "Please allow me to clean up the mess I've made."

With that he softly licked off the chocolate from her now aching body. Her nipples had become so hard and she desperately needed him to suck them. She grabbed his head and guided his mouth to them. When ……….

"Mum, Dad its Lloyd!" yelled a voice from downstairs. "Did you forget about me? Good job I met Bills mam was at the station."

"Fuck!" cried Megan flopping back with her head in her hands.

"You said it love" said Paul.

Megan jumped out of bed quickly putting on her dressing gown and made her way downstairs. She left Paul to hide the evidence and to calm down so to speak.

"Is it the 10th already! Gosh sorry I must have over slept" Megan explained hurriedly.

"God Mam you're turning into a teenager. Standards are obviously slipping since I have left home then" said Lloyd laughing.

"Oh come yer my little man give yer mam a cwtch. Welcome home" said Megan who despite the circumstances was still happy seeing her strong handsome long haired son safely home.

"Ah it's good to be home mam" sighed Lloyd.

"Out of the way of the door man" shouted Angharad as she walked into the hall.

"O Lloydo welcome home man" she said as she gave him a big hug.

This caused Megan to smile at Paul as he begrudgingly made his way back down stairs. This was the closest she had seen her children as they were usually trying to kill one another.

"Hi dad" said Lloyd.

"Welcome home son, when you having your haircut then you scruffy oik" joked Paul.

Lloyd had always wanted grow his hair long but his school wouldn't allow it, so as soon as he was accepted into university his reluctant visits to the barbers ceased.

"Come on Lloydo tell me about Newcastle, got any good clubs there?" asked Angharad putting her arm around his neck guiding him to the living room.

Paul came to the bottom of the stairs grabbing Megan by the belt of her dressing gown which caused it to open. He pulled her naked body to him and gave her a big kiss.

"I love you Meg, my my mad wife" said Paul gleefully.

"Perhaps we can try again after Christmas?" asked Megan hopefully.

"It's a date" said Paul "Come on woman get some bacon on I'm starving!" he joked as he playfully smacked her bottom. Megan squealed with joy as she did up her dressing gown and headed for the kitchen.

CHAPTER 14

SCHOOLS OUT FOR CHRISTMAS

Arriving back in work on Monday morning she had Billie, Seren and Max waiting in her office. "So?" they asked expectantly.

"I don't want to talk about it but I will just say that Lloyd came home" said Megan.

"Oh god he didn't catch you at it on the kitchen table did he?" said Max in horror.

"No cos there was no kitchen table, nothing happened" said Megan sternly.

"What nothing!" exclaimed Billie disappointed?

"Nothing, now back to work please "said Megan sternly.

As it was the run up to Christmas it was the best week of school for the kids, staff and families. There was reception school's nativity, the juniors carol concert by candle light in the local church. There were party and games for the kids till they broke up.

On the last day of term when school had finished for Christmas all the staff went over to the Crows Tavern after work for a festive drink. There was a live band playing so the atmosphere jovial and relaxed.

Mr Evans bought the first round for everyone to say thank you for all their hard work and Megan helped serve the drinks.

"Oh Megan "said Mr Evans "I think I saw you on the station the other day when I was picking up my wife, I saw a new side of you I must say."

"Oh I can explain" began Megan flustered.

"Oh I don't think you need to do that. I am a wise old monkey you know, see no evil, hear no evil etc." said Mr Evans smiling smugly.

"Thanks" said Megan feeling a bit wary about being beholden to Mr Evans.

So after a few vodkas, Megan told Billie, Seren and Max about the fiasco at the train station and they laughed like drains.

"Three cheers for Megan!" they cheered wiping the tears of laughter from their eyes.

Then the band played "Last Christmas" "could I have this dance Mrs Jones" asked Max politely.

"Why of course Master Abraham" said Megan smiling.

Max took Megan in his arms and they danced together slowly. Megan held her breath as she was in his arms again.

"I know we danced to "Careless Whisper" last time but anything by George Michael is good" said Max.

"You remembered" said Megan in surprise.

"Of course "said Max. "Everything about that night is etched in my memory forever."

"Oh "said Megan a little taken aback.

"Tell me Megan, are you happy?" asked Max earnestly.

"Yes I am very happy with Paul. Thanks Max" said Megan smiling.

"Just wanted to make sure" said Max.

Then music suddenly stopped as the barman took the mic to make an announcement.

"Just to let you know that Jayne Goodwin has had a 9lb baby boy today!"

Everyone cheered and Mr Evans bought another round of drinks which was a miracle in itself.

Paul pulled up outside the pub to collect Megan. She gave Billie and Seren a kiss and hug goodbye. Then found herself standing in front of Max. He took her hands gently, sighed and looked at her with his piercing blue eyes which Megan could not be entranced by.

He leaned forward and whispered in her ear,

 "Have a wonderful Christmas, Megan."

This sent shivers down her spine, causing an involuntary spasm of her pelvic muscles. Then he kissed her cheek which she was forced to restrain from kissing him passionately back. A tear trickled down her cheek, as she thought another time another day things could have been.

"Are you ok Megan?" he asked concerned.

"You're not real, you are a fantasy, and I'm too old for you. Find someone and have beautiful babies" said Megan, then she pulled away frightened of the feelings that stirred within her by Max. She turned away from Max and ran towards Paul's waiting car shouting back "Merry Christmas everyone".

"Merry Christmas "was the return cry from everyone.

"Hi love, had a good time?" asked Paul as he started the car.

"Yes lovely thanks" said Megan.

She quickly looked in the glove compartment for a pack of tissues and laughed to herself with relief when she found some. She then took a tissue out wiped her eyes and blew her nose.

"You crying?" asked Paul concerned.

"Oh it's the drink, I must have drunk too much, sorry" said Megan.

"That's what Christmas is all about isn't it?" said Paul softly.

As they drove off they passed Billie and Max walking with linked arms merrily singing Christmas carols.

"Who's that with Billie I haven't seen him before?"

"Oh that's just Max, he's the supply teacher for Jayne. Oh Jayne had a baby boy it was announced tonight" said Megan trying to change the subject.

"He is a good looking young man don't you think Meg?" asked Paul suspiciously.

"I suppose so, he lives with Billie" Megan answered quickly.

Which was the truth in a way? She consoled herself.

Which thankfully made Paul visibly relaxed "Ok then let's get you home."

Megan felt relieved but couldn't help feeling guilty about having to lie to him.

CHAPTER 15

CHRISTMAS

As the Sunday dinners were proving very popular at Otter Shell Restaurant her eldest son Iestyn decided to offer the regulars the opportunity to make reservations for Christmas dinner. For this they charged a huge price in order to make it exclusive and much to Iestyn's excitement they swiftly sold out.

This being the case Megan and Paul decided the only way to see Iestyn over Christmas was for them to drive the family to Brighton on Christmas morning. The bonus for Megan that she was off the hook for her to create her usual Christmas disaster.

How many times had she found after the meal was finished that the sprouts were still in the microwave or the stuffing still in the oven. This year she felt she could now relax and look forward to Christmas dinner in the company of her family. She was so excited that they were going to be all together for Christmas.

On Christmas morning Paul parked outside Iestyn's apartment building and put the permit Iestyn had posted them in the windscreen. Leaving the presents in the car they made their way to the restaurant. The quirky seaside themed restaurant had washed up wood and shells adorned everywhere and even had a stuffed seagull on the bar. This style was accessorised with beads, lace voiles and pretty pastel glasses containing tea lights which enhanced the red and gold Christmas decorations.

We were warmly welcomed by the owner Crystal. Who was attractive, tall, slim, blonde and beautiful. She wore a simple short plain red dress and ankle boots which showed off her toned legs. She was gorgeous and totally smitten with the tall dark handsome Iestyn. Crystal had the perfect laid back style accompanied by a brilliant business brain which helped loosen Iestyn's uptight perfectionist persona. He excitedly came out of the kitchen in his chef white jacket, black and white check trousers and, showing Crystal's influence Megan thought, had a brightly coloured bandanna covering his short dark hair to greet his family glowing with happiness. This filled Megan and Paul with warm satisfied joy as they automatically hugged each other filled with pride then suddenly released each other self-consciously.

"Wow Megan I love your hair, you look amazing!" announced Crystal as she help with their coats.

Megan had worn a black trouser suit with a lace vest top. She blushed with embarrassment at this sudden attention but enjoyed the praise as everyone agreed with Crystal.

"How's my little sis after the aftermath of "he who can't be named?" asked Iestyn giving her a big hug.

"Oh I'm getting there" said Angharad enjoying being wrapped in her big brother's arms.

"Well at least you got a free holiday to Canada out of that relationship" he added jokingly. "That's not to be sniffed at!"

"Oh trust you to think of that" she said laughing and breaking away.

"Come now everyone take a seat, I need to get back to the kitchen I have a masterpiece to prepare" said Iestyn seemly a little testy all of a sudden.

"Oh go on, back in the kitchen with you" joked Crystal as she playfully kissed his cheek and pushed him away. "He gets so wound up" she whispered when he was out of earshot, then cheerfully announced "Drink anyone."

Christmas songs were playing in the background making the atmosphere cosy warm and friendly. The mouth-watering delicious food was impeccably served by Crystal and Cat the waitress accompanied with lots of wine. Iestyn of course, checked between courses to check for everyone's approval.

Megan looked across the table and proudly admired her family. Opposite her was Angharad's fresh face glowing in the candle light with her strawberry blonde uncontrollable curly hair which she had tried to tame with a ponytail but always had escaping curls. She still had a light dusting of freckles to remind Megan of the little girl she used to be. She wore a little blusher, mascara and lip gloss. She wore a patterned green and red tunic with black leggings with long black boots. This showed she had put a real effort into looking good today as she had sacrificed her usual tracksuit and trainers, which pleased Megan. It was nice to see her looking so grown up, attractive, feminine and clean.

On the other hand Lloyd with hair long looked more like Tarzan every day, Megan thought which made her smile. Although his thick dark wavy hair which framed an unshaven face at least he was wearing white open necked shirt with a waistcoat and black jeans, so Megan was gratified that he had made a some effort to look nice too.

Everyone in the restaurant seemed relaxed and chatted away happily to each other while they ate.

Then Paul caught her eye, through the soft candle light Megan thought how attractive Paul looked tonight.

Even in his Christmas jumper, that he wore every year since her mum had bought it for him, did not detract from his handsome features. If they had created this wonderful family surely they could be ok?

After the meal Crystal busily helped the other guests with their coats and took the money to settle their bills. Cat served the family fresh coffee and brandy to finish off the meal.

"Iestyn won't be long" reassured Cat.

Then Crystal gave Cat a Christmas present and a big hug.

"Thanks Cat for working today, now go home and have a great night with your family" said Crystal earnestly. "We are not open again till well into the new year so enjoy your rest."

"Thanks and Merry Christmas" replied Cat and wrapped up warm against the bitter chill outside.

Crystal slumped down in a chair and drank some brandy with the family.

"You look exhausted" said Angharad.

"How much do we owe you Crystal?" asked Paul reaching for his wallet.

"Gosh don't be mad!" exclaimed Crystal, "Put your money away, we're almost family."

At that juncture Iestyn joined them at the table with a glass of red wine, a plate of grapes and big chunk of stilton.

"Yes it has its perks sleeping with the boss" he said cheekily kissing Crystal's cheek.

"Look at him, a brilliant chef but still loves his cheese. Oh it's so nice for you to come today, my family are not close at all. But all I get from Iestyn is Nan used to say this, Mum says that and of course Dad does this. Its lovely, best decision of my life, hiring Iestyn as my chef!" She exclaimed.

"I'll drink to that!" said Iestyn and they all joined in the toast.

"And Mexico here we come!" Iestyn continued.

"Yes two whole weeks in Mexico" agreed Crystal. "I can't wait."

"Oh perhaps it was asking too much you putting us up for Christmas?" asked Megan concerned.

"No don't be silly, we've been looking forward to it. Come on let's get out of here!" exclaimed Crystal. They all quickly cleared the table and took the tray full of coffee cups and glasses to the kitchen followed by Iestyn.

They all put on their coats and woollens and fuel by the Christmas spirit (and the alcohol) sang Christmas carols as they walked to the apartment. Angharad grabbed Pauls arm and Lloyd grabbed Megan's. Megan wondered how much longer Lloyd would want to be so close to his mother as she saw Iestyn cwtched up with Crystal.

Angharad and Paul retrieved the presents from the car. They had a lovely night with a beautiful buffet that Iestyn had prepared for them in advance and exchanging gifts. The air was filled with laughter and happiness as Paul and Megan sat together on the settee. Iestyn had bought everyone pyjamas as Megan had always done for them as children.

"Christmas eve was always bath, new pyjamas and bed, willing ourselves to sleep waiting for Father Christmas to arrive" chorused Iestyn, Angharad and Lloyd.

Paul put his arms around Megan as they watched the family they had created excitedly exchange and open gifts with sounds of glee and surprise. It felt so natural and warm.

How could they throw what they had away? Megan thought.

CHAPTER 16

NEW YEAR

Every year Paul's family had an open house party for New Year's Eve as it was also Paul's dad's birthday. Megan and Paul's mother Patricia had the sort of relationship that only involved speaking politely to each other for Paul's sake. Angharad managed to duck out of the party this year as she was going out with Amy and Iestyn was in sunny Mexico with Crystal. So that left poor Lloyd to come along and put up with the cousins.

Paul was the most successful one in his family and he was the only one who went to university and ran a successful business. Instead of his family being proud they resented him and blamed Megan and her high and mighty ways for losing Paul from the clan's grip.

This meant the only time Paul saw his family was every New Year, so there is no getting out of it for Megan. Who found the evening always a huge effort to be calm and polite. Paul disappear with his brothers and the blow up bed at the end of the night was the only thing Megan looked forward to.

But this year Paul hardly left Megan's side and introduced her into the conversation as if it was her first visit. Paul also kept reassuringly touching Megan as they laughed together with his family.

Then when "Robbie Williams's record "she's the one" came on, Paul took Megan's hand asked her in front of his family, "Could I have this dance please."

"Of course, I would love to dance with you" said Megan laughing.

Paul took her in his arms, Megan thought how nice it was nice to be holding each other so close. Megan put her head on his shoulder and breathed in his Hugo Boss aftershave kissed his neck gently. Then moved her head so their noses were touching.

"Thanks Meg for coming here every year with the children and putting up with my family on your own. I realise now how I used ignore you to drink with my brothers. I am so sorry Meg that I have taken you for granted" said a regretful Paul tears welling in his eyes.

"Hey that's ok, it works both ways because you put up with my family too "said Megan taken back at this sudden show of emotion from Paul.

"Oh love there is no comparison with your family. I loved your mum and dad and I miss your mum every day. She told

me to hang on and that you would come back to me. She had faith in us till the end did Gwen, love her. "

They both danced slowly with tears in their eyes as they realised the love for each other still there.

"Happy New Year Megan."

"Happy New Year Paul"

They kissed each other softly and affectionately, awakening the feelings inside that bringing them closer together.

Morning could not come fast enough for Megan and Paul, who had struggled to sleep on the moving airbed all night in the middle of the living room surrounded by snoring drunken bodies on chairs , settee's and strewn around the floor in sleeping bags. They felt as if they were like refugees clinging onto a raft adrift at sea. They quietly tiptoed around the sleeping bodies and got dressed hurriedly in the bathroom. They decided between them to come back for Lloyd later wherever he was amongst the bodies.

They quietly carried all their things out to the car as if they were escaping from prison. They sat in the car looked at each other and both gave a huge sigh of relief to be going home.

They let themselves in slumped on the settee relieved and tired that the ordeal was over for another year.

"Cup of tea?" asked Paul nuzzling Megan's neck.

This awoke Megan's desire making her want Paul to kiss her more.

"Shall we go to bed?" asked Megan suggestively.

"Oh what a good idea" said Paul.

They ran upstairs giggling only unexpectedly find Angharad's door open and a half asleep naked Max leaving her room.

"Max!" Megan cried out in shock.

"Oh Christ, Megan!" Max cried out covering his crown jewels with his hands. "You….you live here?" he added in a squeaky voice of disbelief.

"Who the fuck are you and what are you doing in my home?" shouted an angry Paul.

Angharad came to her bedroom door in her dressing gown with her hair and makeup everywhere, "Chill dad he's with me "said Angharad sleepily.

Megan and Max froze to the spot staring at each other not knowing what to do. Then Paul broke the spell as he said to Megan gently, "Come on I think we need that strong cup of tea now love."

"Yes "Megan managed to mumble.

 She felt she had been in a road traffic accident. Unable to

understand her feelings or the sudden situation she found herself in, she blindly followed Paul downstairs.

Max hurriedly got dressed and gave Angharad a kiss on the cheek.

"You don't have to run off I'm sure my parents are cool about"

"No, they have had a shock, its best I go "said Max determinedly. "I'll call you."

"Ok" said Angharad.

"Bye Mr and Mrs Jones" he called out as he left sheepishly.

Megan made her way to the downstairs toilet and silently cried. The fantasy she had created making her feel young and desirable was totally destroyed, she suddenly felt old and exhausted.

"I'm sorry Paul, do you mind if I take a rain check on the tea. I've got a thumping headache and I think I'll just go to bed. "

"Yes of course love, a bit of a shock eh. It was bound to happen sometime suppose. I always thought it would be Iestyn that would do this to us" said Paul softly.

"Yeah Kids eh?" said Megan, trying so sound ok instead of the rejected old woman that she felt she was. It took all her effort to crawl into bed. "Oh well tomorrows another day…." She said to herself.

CHAPTER 17

REGRETS

After the Christmas break Megan returned to work to find Max in her office with a cup of coffee and a repentant chocolate muffin.

"Sorry Megan" he started.

"I don't want to hear it" said Megan harshly putting up her hand to stop him in his tracks. "And don't think for a minute that muffin is going to make this ok. This is too fucked up even for Freud. "

"But Megan, I didn't know who she was!" reasoned Max.

"What has that got to do with the price of fish? You little using shit. She was vulnerable. She just had her heart broken" shouted Megan.

"I know, she told me, we both had that in common Megan. My hearts been kicked around lately too" Implored Max.

Megan suddenly remembered Max's recent heart break.

"Sorry I guess I have been a bit self-absorbed lately" said Megan quietly

"Look if it's any consolation she dumped me straight away as she's going back to university and doesn't want a relationship. It was just a bit of fun. In my view I am the one who has been used and casually cast aside by both of you and it's not doing my confidence any good I can tell you. "

"Oh Max I get your point" said Megan "I'll take the coffee and muffin after all. I'm sure there is someone out there for you."

"Thanks Megan, but I'll make sure I keep away from the wild Jones women in future" Max sighed as he left her office.

Eating the muffin and coffee brought a smile to her face in the knowledge that Angharad had grown into a strong self-assured woman.

There is no way she would have had the willpower to kick such a handsome young man into touch when she was that young. God am I that twisted I am proud of my daughter for using a handsome Englishman or maybe he was just shit in bed. Megan your thoughts are becoming shameful girl. She chastised herself then smiled wickedly, "Wild Jones women eh?"

CHAPTER 18

A GREAT ADVENTURE

Megan's case was all packed and waiting in her car. She had bought new clothes and underwear for this trip. The tickets mysteriously had come in the post by special delivery with an anonymous letter enclosed with instructions.

"Are you ready then Hunny?" asked Billie.

"Yes," said Megan excitedly.

The school bell rang for end of Friday's lessons.

"Good luck!" squealed Billie giving Megan a big kiss and hug.

Mr Evans walked in "Right Megan, just want to go through these figures."

"I'm sorry" said Billie "But she has a plane to catch. Go on Megan I'll sort this out for you. Just go!"

"Thanks "said Megan thrilled, grabbed her handbag, ran to the car and sped off to the airport at full speed. Thinking to herself *I'm going to have sex tonight!*

The car had been prebooked into the car park so Megan made the flight easily with plenty of time to spare. She sat on the plane excitedly re-reading the instructions that were

sent to her. She landed at Edinburgh Airport and got a taxi to the Royal Mile. The taxi took her to the Grand Hotel and she walked confidently into reception in her beige mac *full clothed underneath this time.*

 "Hello I 'm Miss Megan Cassagrande, I believe there is an envelope left here for me" Megan asked the receptionist.

"Yes of course, here you are Miss Cassagrande, have a nice day" said the smiling receptionist as she passed the envelope to her.

Megan impatiently ripped the envelope open to find a key card for room 424 with a typed note saying:

"**Make yourself comfortable.**

 Then meet me in the hotel bar 7.30 pm".

Megan found her way went to the room number 424 as directed in the note.

Megan's heart raced as she opened the room door to find herself in a luxury suite. On further inspection Megan discovered a large chilled bottle of prosecco in an ice bucket and beautiful vase of flowers. She smiled and sniffed the flowers taking in its beautiful fragrance, then poured herself a large glass of prosecco. *Ooh this is nice I could get us to this* she thought.

She went to the bathroom and decided to have a warm leisurely bubble bath from the complimentary basket provided.

She then changed into a red cocktail dress, black shoes and clutch bag. She added another layer of vivid red lipstick as she apprehensively made her way down the Hotel Bar. She had never walked into a bar unaccompanied before.

Her mother was probably turning in her grave at her daughters loose morals she thought to herself.

She calmly sat at the bar and ordered a martini trying to pretend this was an everyday occurrence for her. A dark handsome man approached her like a tiger swooping on his prey.

"Hello, could I buy you a drink?"

Megan felt a rush of excitement replied "No thanks, I have one already."

Then a familiar voice whispered in her ear "do you come here often?"

She turned to reply "No"

There stood Paul looking very relaxed and confident in a black suit and white shirt oozing sex appeal which took Megan's breath away.

"I had to be quick, as you look so hot, Then I thought you wouldn't be left drinking alone for long" said Paul saucily.

"Ooh you know how to say all the right things" purred Megan.

"If I may, our table is ready m'lady" said Paul offering his arm.

"Why thank you kind sir" replied Megan.

They made their way to the hotel restaurant. The table was indeed ready with champagne on ice waiting for them. The waiter poured champagne for them while Paul ordered they're meal. Instead of moaning to each other about their day, they had a delightful evening. Paul talked about his successful meetings in Edinburgh and Megan explained her job as a school secretary in glowing terms to impress Paul. They both shared each other's hopes and dreams. It seemed there was nobody else in the restaurant as they were totally engrossed in each other, each looking admiringly across the candlelit table. Every accidental brush of the hand built up the electricity between them so they decided to skip desert and they made their way to the suite.

"After you m'lady" said Paul as he opened the door for her.

"Thank you kind sir" said Megan as she entered the suite.

Paul followed and poured two large brandies. Megan took a big gulp of the brandy then quickly turned away as she nearly choked fortunately managed kept her calm demeanour by walking determinedly towards Paul, cupped his face in her hands and kissed him slowly and longingly.

"Wow" said Paul.

He put his glass down and gently kissed Megan's neck while slowly undoing her zip.

"I have been waiting to take this dress off all night!" he whispered as he kissed her smooth skin gently and lightly.

She took a sharp intake of breath when he reached her lower back with his kisses and her dress fell to the floor.

She stood there in her red sheer lacy underwear, stockings and suspenders and her black high heeled shoes. Paul's eyes lit up with desire, he took her in his arms and kissed her deeply and their tongues toyed and teased with each other. Their pelvises were held together by a magnetic force. Then Paul pushed Megan roughly away so she landed on the bed causing her to giggle. Paul took off his shirt with his lustful eyes locked on Megan.

"Now Miss Cassagrande, do you know what I'm going to do to you?" Paul said as he undressed.

"No" Megan manged to reply as her desire for him heightened.

He gently and slowly removed her lacy pants, slowly kissed her warm wet vagina. She moaned with every artful stroke of his tongue on her clitoris. Then suddenly the fire alarm went off.

"Holy fuck!" shouted Paul jumping up. "I don't fucking believe this!"

Megan could have cried as she was so desperate for Paul. They both grabbed the white dressing gown and slippers that the hotel provided and begrudgingly made their way down the fire escape and waited patiently outside with all the rest of the guests for the fire service to come.

"Oh my god, this would be so fucking ironic if it wasn't so fucking annoying!" shouted Paul.

This caused Megan to laugh till tears fell from the eyes and Paul could not help but join in. They both looked a curious sight stood there dressing gowns laughing hysterically for all to see in freezing cold in the middle of Edinburgh in January waiting to be let back into the hotel.

All Megan could say "I can't believe I'm standing here with no knickers on. "

They both laughed hysterically trying to stop their dressing gowns from loosening until the fire service arrived and gave them foil blankets as they waited for them to say it was safe to return inside.

When they eventually got the all clear Paul and Megan resignedly headed for the bar to get more brandy to defrost themselves before heading for bed.

The next morning Megan put on the magic knickers she had bought that made you look two sizes slimmer so she could wear a black woollen figure hugging dress and long boots. They had full cooked breakfast and got wrapped up as Paul had booked a trip to Edinburgh Castle.

As they walked around the castle they noticed they had automatically started holding hands, they both looked at each other thinking why something so natural had become so rare for them.

Then Megan started to have stomach pains which she tried to ignore but the pain would not desist, then she started to sweat. Paul noticing Megan's grey face asked "Are you ok love?"

"Yes, I think so" replied Megan but then found she could hardly walk any further.

"What's wrong love, tell me?" begged Paul.

"Umm well I bought these magic knickers so wear this dress and look sexy for you but they are killing me "said Megan embarrassed.

"Take them off then" said Paul pragmatically.

"No, I can't walk around Edinburgh with no bloody knickers on!" Megan protested in a panic.

"Well it's better than being in pain" said Paul.

"No I just can't!" said Megan in despair.

"I know" suggested Paul "Why you don't wear my boxers as I'm wearing trousers."

"Ok "Megan agreed out of desperation.

Paul went into the men's lavatory and returned with his boxers screwed up in his hand and passed them to Megan discreetly. Megan headed to the ladies cubicle the relief was immediate when Megan took off the "magic" knickers and quickly put on Paul's boxers which felt far more comfortable. She joyously jammed the offending knickers into the sanitary bin, as she never wanted to see them again. Smiling with relief Megan re- joined Paul,

"Oh you look so much better now love "said Paul.

"Thank you so much" said Megan "sorry for spoiling the day."

"No problem" said Paul laughing. "It's not every day that I get to go commando and you, you hussy going around Edinburgh castle with my pants on, is that purvey or what."

They both laughed and carried on with the tour.

That evening Megan got ready as Paul had booked a five star Tai restaurant called "Lucky No. 9" for a treat that evening.

She put on her black lacy cocktail dress, black lacy hold ups and finished the look with her red heels, to match her red

lipstick. She felt very sexy and daring and she couldn't wait to go out again. She couldn't believe she was having so much fun with Paul.

Once ready she left the bathroom to enter the room.

Paul exclaimed "Wow, you look amazing! "Which made Megan's heart skip a beat.

Paul wore a red shirt on with black jacket and trousers. He looked so handsome she found him hard to resist but she wanted the evening to be perfect so she fought back her building passion. Instead she took his arm and accompanied him to the taxi which was waiting to take them to the restaurant.

They were welcomed at the restaurant by a Tai lady who took their coats and showed them to some leather settees while they waited for their table. Paul ordered a bottle of champagne,

"I could get use to this life "he said relaxing on the settee.

Megan on the other hand felt awkward as she had to sit on the very edge of the settee and keep pulling her dress down as her dress rode up making her stocking tops visible to all.

"Are you ok love, is it your tummy again?" asked Paul concerned.

"No, I have never sat down in these stockings with this dress on" whispered Megan. "I'm so sorry."

She could feel the confident Megan was melting away making the awkward Mrs Jones steadily reappear.

"Hey love drink your champagne and try to relax. I'm sure everyone is too absorbed in each other rather than looking at your extremely sexy stockings" said Paul smiling. "Thank you by the way."

"For what?" Megan asked confused.

"Buying them for me" he said smiling.

"Hey I bought them for myself Mister, so don't get so cocky" said Megan haughtily but smiling.

"But I thought that was the point of the evening" said Paul laughing wickedly.

They both started laughing again.

"This champagnes good" Megan purred.

"No it's your sparkling company" said Paul.

Megan then noticed his blue eyes were sparkling.

"Thank you Paul, for all this, you are so lush. I'm so enjoying tonight" said Megan earnestly.

Paul poured two more glasses of champagne

"I'll drink to that "he said. Raising his glass he toasted "Hers to being happy."

"Being happy" Megan cheered and they clinked glasses.

 When ready the beautiful Thai lady showed them to their table. Megan's heart sunk, there was no table cloth! Which meant her stocking tops would be on show. Then as she sat down awkwardly in order to stop them showing one came unstuck and started falling down. Megan could have cried as she felt as was ruining this wonderful evening.

"Are you sure you're ok?" asked Paul.

"Yes it's lovely. It's just that …. When did tablecloths go out of fashion?"

"Why, don't you like it here?"

"No, it's just that one of my stockings has come unstuck. I think I should get in touch with trading standards as these are not holding up. Don't worry I'll just have to eat with one hand "

"You can't eat a meal holding on to your stocking all night. Look love thanks for the thought, but all I want is for you to have a good time, so take them off" suggested Paul.

"You don't mind?"

"No of course not. It's you I want to get into not your stockings" Paul added saucily.

"Thanks" said Megan gratefully.

"I'll order for you if you like"

Megan gave her stocking a big tug and made her way holding up her one stocking through her dress as she walked awkwardly to the ladies. Megan's heart sunk as there seemed to be a queue of young well-dressed ladies.

"Are you alright" said a blonde young Scottish woman looking concerned at Megan's slightly hunched gate.

The champagne must have kicked in as Megan replied "Well, I'm having a right mare of a night. My husband's taking me out for this special meal right, and look" as she let go of her stocking and it fell to her ankle.

The girls started to laugh, "Oh love "

"I know "Megan implored "I'm spoiling the night and he is so lush he is."

The flush went and a stunning woman opened the cubicle door.

"I know that accent anywhere, are you Welsh?" asked the stunning Scottish lady.

Oh she must be, she sounds so cute. She sounds like "Gavin and Stacy "she even said lush" said the first blonde girl.

"I love Wales" said the lady as she washed her hands. "I went to Cardiff University, best time of my life. Och I love the welsh."

"Yeah, I live not far from Cardiff" replied Megan.

"My names Kirsty, its Aileen's hen night tonight so we are starting the night off ere! So what are we going to do with this stocking hen?"

"Oh I was just going to take them off" replied Megan.

"Och you ney want to do that lass. You softy southerner wouldn't survive January up here without your stockings" said one of the girls.

"Hey she's a Celt isn't she? Anyway these stockings are expensive so we can't have you wasting them."

"This has happened to me, you just add water the top of the stocking and they re-stick."

With that the three girls were pushing her to the sink. Much to Megan's astonishment and amusement they had their hands up underneath her dress getting the stocking top wet and to Megan's grateful surprise they managed to get the stocking to stay up.

"Well thanks very much that's tidy that is" said Megan to the girl's amusement.

Another girl popped her head in the loos "Come on Aileen," which prompted the rest of the girls burst into a chorus of "Come on Aileen!" by Dexy's midnight Runners.

"Hey I've been helping a welsh lady in distress!" laughed Aileen.

"If you want to catch us up with us later we are off to Old Mother Hubbard's Karaoke bar next" suggested Kirsty.

"Hey, she don't want to be with us. She's got 'er lush husband remember?" said Aileen.

"I know, I want to see a lush husband" added Kirsty laughing.

Then they all in turn hugged and kissed Megan goodbye, wished her luck and went off singing "Come on Aileen!"

Megan was well chuffed by the Scottish girl's kindness and she returned to her table confidently.

"Bloody hell you were ages was there a long queue?" asked Paul as Megan's Green Thai Soup had already been served.

"Long story" she replied smiling and started her soup.

"Well you look loads better so well done for fixing your stocking" added Paul.

"Yes the people here are lovely" said Megan beaming.

They carried on with the main course of steamed fish and Jasmine rice.

"I thought you didn't like fish?" asked Megan.

"Well when in Rome, I'm trying to be more adventurous for you love" said Paul. "Meg I've been meaning to ask you, what are you going to do with your house in Portugal? You haven't touched it since Avo left it to you, it's been years love. Do you think you should go over to Portugal just to see what condition it's in?"

"I know, I will have to bring myself to go" agreed Megan. "I can't ignore it any more. I have to accept that Avo, mam, dad, they are all are gone and I need to decide what needs to be done."

"Well I'm glad you're feeling strong enough to even talk about it" said Paul gently and touched Megan's hand. "If you want I could sell the business and we could move out there. Fresh start so to speak, I've realised how much I have missed you Meg and I want to make the most of you while we still have each other."

"I know my dad was only forty when he first got ill……." Said Megan choking on her words as the tears threatened to fall.

"I know love, so let's do it, let's go to Portugal" coaxed Paul.

"I'll see love. Don't make me cry tonight. I don't want to cry tonight"

"Ok subject over, new one please" said Paul smiling.

So Megan told Paul about what happened in the ladies as they ate dessert Khanom Chan which made them laugh. They were still laughing when the coffees came.

"Thank you Paul that was lush" said Megan.

"So Megan there is a decision to be made "he said suddenly seriously. "Would you like to go to Mother Hubbard's Karaoke Bar, or would you prefer a night cap back at the hotel?"

"Oh I don't know, it's a tough decision" teased Megan. "It depends on whether you are going to take advantage of me or not?"

"Oh I can guarantee I will be on my worst behaviour" replied Paul suggestively.

"Ooh in that case let's get to the hotel room quickly" said Megan cheekily.

So they got a taxi and made their way back to the hotel.

"Thanks love I felt like a princess tonight" said Megan as she cwtched into Paul in the taxi.

"Hey the night isn't over yet" promised Paul.

Megan smile excitedly in reply.

They made their way through reception and up the lift to the room. Then Paul opened the door and rushed to the loo to be violently sick.

"Are you ok?" asked Megan through the door.

"No" Paul managed to say as he continued to vomit.

"Anything, I can do love"

"Noooo"

So Megan took her make up off at the dressing table and got changed into her black nightie as Paul serenaded her with his vomiting groans. In a lull in the proceedings, Megan then popped her head around the door.

She asked gently "Do you want anything love?"

"I suppose a shag is out of the question?" asked Paul laughing before vomiting again.

"I don't think so love "Megan replied laughing and gave him a glass of water.

"I'm so sorry love" said Paul between bouts of vomiting "I'll never eat fish again" he moaned.

"Well I had the same as you love and I'm ok. But don't worry Hun" said Megan smiling to herself nestling in bed with a cup of tea watching the TV.

CHAPTER 19

ALONE AT LAST

Megan and Paul both arrived back at their house at the same time.

"Well fancy seeing you here" said Megan. "Have a good weekend?"

"Well I have had better!" mumbled Paul.

"How are you feeling now love?" asked Megan opening the front door.

"Ok, just a little tender" answered Paul and dropped his bags in the hallway. "Listen!" he added.

"I can't hear anything" said Megan.

"Exactly, silence" said Paul with his eyes closed standing still.

Megan just looked at him curiously and dropped her bags too.

He opened his eyes and put his finger to his lips "Shh."

He then ran upstairs and went around all the rooms shouting "Hellooo, hello is there anybody there."

Then he ran downstairs and much to Megan's amusement he checked all the rooms downstairs too.

"You know "whispered Paul" I think we're alone."

"Ooh so what are we going to do?" asked Megan excitedly.

"Well "ordered Paul "You can get up them stairs now woman!"

Megan squealed, "Oh I love you when you are being so forceful" and ran up the stairs with Paul chasing her, watching her round bottom wobble with glee.

"Are you naked yet wench?" shouted Paul.

"Not yet" said Megan laughing as she hurriedly striped off her clothes. Paul tore his clothes off too.

Then without candles, wine, or soft music they just did it. Megan laid back on the bed then Paul pinned her hands above her head and inserted his hard erection into a desperate and wanton Megan. Then they fucked hard and fast releasing all their pent up frustration.

Megan's worries about her weight and stretch marks as she felt free, wild and wanton.

Paul forgot about his lack of hair and his age. He felt young, hard and filled with animal lust.

"They did it like the discovery channel", as the song goes.

Then they did it in the bathroom, they did it in the kitchen, then they had a cup of tea in bed.

"Ahh we still got it haven't we "said Paul.

"Yes Love" replied Megan. "We've still got it babe."

"Fancy another go?"

"Ooh yes please!"

"We haven't done it in the living room, yet."

"But the settee is cream!" shrieked Megan.

"Oh fuck the settee!" Paul groaned in disappointment fearing that the spell was broken and sensible Megan had returned.

"No Babe fuck me not the settee!" Megan said wickedly grabbing his hand as they ran downstairs.

The next morning they overslept lost in wonderful deep post coital sleep. Suddenly there was banging on the front door which woke them up with a start

They put on their dressing gowns and made their way downstairs to open the door to Angharad, who shouted "Why did you leave the key in the door? I couldn't get in. God its brass monkeys out here. Dad did you hire the van to move me, cos my mates were asking?"

She was then followed by Lloyd moaning "I don't know if I'm on the right course. Do you think university is a good idea? Put the kettle on mum, what do you think I should do?"

Lloyd was closely followed by Iestyn and Crystal who announced "We had to come straight away to tell you the news, we are so excited! We are having a baby!"

"Sod the tea mam where is the prosecco?" exclaimed Angharad "Congratulations!" she shouted as she hugged them both.

The front doorbell went again this time Megan found Billie at the door.

"Is everything ok?" asked Megan worried.

"I need to talk to you" said Billie seriously.

"Of course come through to the living room" said Megan apprehensive to hear Billie's news.

"Well" said Billie. "I had to tell you, please don't hate me, but I slept with Max last night" she spluttered out.

"Oh thank god!" cried Megan in relief.

"Pardon?" said Billie in surprise.

"I thought it was going to be something serious then. That's brilliant Billie, you will make a lovely couple, honestly" said Megan in delight.

"You don't mind?" asked Billie unsure.

"Of course not. I love Paul. You couldn't have made me happier except, I have just been told I'm going to be a granny! Come and join us for a drink "begged Megan as she made her way back to the joyful commotion in the kitchen.

"Angharad please get Billie a drink" asked Megan.

"What about the restaurant?" asked Paul.

"Oh yes I'm sure grandpa and grandma can help us" said Iestyn

Megan and Paul looked across the room at one another in horror.

"Portugal?" asked Paul over the noise and excitement.

"Yes please!" said Megan.

"I'll book the flights for next week."

They both took each other in their arms and kissed.

"Oh man, dad get a room! "Shouted Lloyd. "God they are always at it, honestly. It's disgusting at their age!"

And they all laughed as Megan playfully hit Lloyd over his head.

Megan knew in her heart that even when she moved to Portugal with Paul, she would never lose her family, they would always be a part of each other's life, whatever life holds for them in the future.

THE END or should I say the beginning?

Previous Book By Josephine Jones

TUSK

CHAPTER 1

The cold of the window pane against my head reminded me that I was alive. My thoughts were lost in the multicolored patterns that were in every individual raindrop running down the pane. The sound of "The Cult" whining about the rain grated through my brain. The weather seemed to be a reflection of my life, thanks to Margaret Thatcher, we have entered a dark time. The pit was closed and my father after loyally working down the pit for twenty years was callously thrown on the slag heap himself. So we lost our home, our pride and souls. Now being forced to take refuge at my Nans, which is stressful to all the family to say the least. My Nan unfairly blames my Dad for failing to provide for his family. I am the recipient of most of her moaning, as I am the one who is forced to share a room with her.

The words "Georgina Morgan phone call for you!" suddenly broke me from my thoughts, it was my careers teacher Mr. Burke calling me.

Shit! A phone call at school! Something serious must have happened at home!

I got up and hurriedly followed my teacher to the phone. *I hope Nan's ok. I am always upsetting the family lately. I am already getting close to being thrown out. Why it was only the other week that I took a guy I'd been seeing to my school disco. His name was Ashley. He was a DJ I'd picked up from my mate Julie's 18th birthday party, great dancer, not bad kisser too. It all started well, Ashley and I got there ok and met all my mates, got chatting. We had smuggled in vodka, so only had to buy cokes*

(Which got around the no alcohol policy) Ashley had been getting us the drinks most of the night while we were chatting. Then "Take my breath away" by Berlin began to fill the air.

"Come on Georgina let's dance this is our song!" begged Ashley.

"Our song?" I looked at him quizzically.

"Yes our first date, I took you to see the movie "Top Gun"?"

I looked at my mates. They knew that talk like that had always sent me in a panic. They knew that as soon as any boy tried to get too close I always looked for the way out.

Mam always warned me don't trust men they'll use you. Well the guys round here all seem to be so serious. Where are all the bad guys? I could do with being used.

"Yeah ok" I replied looking at my friend's look of condolence as I accompanied Ashley to the dance floor.

While we smooched to the song I realized that I shouldn't have brought a date to my school disco. It had probably bored him to death. I always keep my love life apart from my school life, as I found boys from school a bit suffocating. I would feel duty bound to see them in school breaks, when all I wanted to do was to hang with my mates.

"Shall we go?" I asked as soon as the song changed. He nodded his agreement. I went to say goodbye to my friends.

"He's nice!" Sian knowingly commented, and under her breath she said "Be kind."

After all the hugs and handshakes goodbye we walked slowly back to my Nan's house.

"Your friends seemed nice?"

"Yeah they are not a bad bunch" I said laughing. "Look I'm really tired, so how are you getting home?"

"I don't know really, can't I stay?" he said leaning in for a kiss.

"Stay! Are you crazy?" I said pushing him away. "Have you met my Mam? My Dad would kill you! Stay! We are overcrowded as it is. I am sharing a room with my Nan for God's sake!" looking around in a panic.

"Look there is a phone box over by there. Why don't you ring for a taxi?"

"I haven't got any change and I don't know any numbers for a taxi" he shrugged smiling. "Couldn't we just go back to yours for a coffee? Perhaps I could use your phone!"

Gosh wish I hadn't drunk so much, I need my wits about me! Right, mental calculation, Mam and Dad sleeping, Nan, if her bladder had held out should be in bed too. I marched off towards the house. Might be able to use the phone quickly to get a taxi before anyone noticed.

"Right ok!" I said begrudgingly "Let's go!"

I was feeling really angry now that he hadn't bothered to think of anyway of going home. I supposed it had always been drummed into me by my parents.

"Where are you going?" "Who with?" and, "How are you getting back?" I was always told, *I thought everyone knew that.*

How many parents would let a boy stay over? Who does he think this is? I Claudius? We had only got as far as snogging. What did he think was going to happen? Bloody hell does this third date myth stuff really happen? Well not with me mate! By the time I had reached my house I was livid. I couldn't leave him stranded could I?

"Right we are here" I whispered, "just be very quiet."

He smiled and nodded with a small laugh, which made me even angrier. Was this a big joke to him? I slowly put the key in the lock and opened the door quietly. I pulled Ashley into the house quickly.

"Georgina is that you?" came a voice from upstairs.

"Shit!" I said under my breath, my mother's radar had been activated. "Yes Mam it's me!" I shouted pushing a quietly laughing Ashley into the dining room.

"Stay here!" I whispered insistently.

Shutting the door and making my way upstairs to my Mam's bedroom.

"Hi Mam" I said trying to be light and airy, as I walked into the flowery pastel explosion of my parents' bedroom.

"Is everything alright? Is there someone with you?" Mam asked accusingly.

She was sat upright in her frilly cotton nighty and rollers in her hair. My dad fast asleep beside.

I have always been useless at lying and so I tried to act as if what I was about to say was the most normal everyday occurrence.

"No Mam Ashley is with me. He is just booking a taxi to take him home. I'm making him a coffee while we wait. Would you like a cup of tea?" I replied with my sweetest smile.

"There…. Is…. A….. BOY…… Down…. Stairs" my mother snarled under her breath.

Her brown eyes looked dark and threatening as she clutching the blankets towards her.

"Yes his name is Ashley! Did you say you would like some tea?" I replied brightly and smiling.

"I do not want a cup of tea! And I don't want a boy in this house Georgina! What would your Nan say?" she hissed

"But!"

"No buts, get him out of the house now!"

Dad stirred.

"It's alright Will" my mother reassured my dad with a little pat. "I don't want you to wake your father. We will discuss this in the morning" she hissed.

With that I was dismissed. I returned downstairs walking through the dining room, without even acknowledging Ashley's existence. I went straight to the kettle and switched it on. While making his coffee, *I thought this was not my fault. I'm going to get it in the neck cos of an idiotic DJ. Who was now kissing my neck and rubbing his body against me. Unbelievable!*

"Right, stop right now!" I cried out, pushing him out of the way. "Here is the phone, here is the phone book, here is my purse and here is your coffee, I have had enough tonight, I'm very tired. You can ring a taxi and just go home. I'm going to bed!" with that I flounced off to bed leaving the bewildered Ashley and, believe it or not went to sleep.

I woke the next morning to my mother screaming. *What the hell was going on!*

"Georgina!" my mother was screaming. "Georgina Morgan get down here now!"

I got up bleary eyed, holding my aching head, while putting my dressing gown on and making my way down towards the noise. To my utter disbelief there standing in my living room was a bewildered Ashley and my horrified Mam.

"What the hell are you still doing here?" I cried incredulously.

"We could have been robbed, murdered in our beds!" my mother was twittering on.

"Calm down now Megan" my dad had just entered the room, in his dressing gown and put his arms gently around my hysterical mother. "Georgina!" he said firmly looking straight at me, as he tried to calm her down.

"Why are you here? I left you the money and the phone. Why didn't you phone a taxi?" I demanded.

"I wanted to find out what I did wrong, why were you so angry? I was waiting for you to come back down" Ashley said softly and calmly.

I felt like such a heel looking at his messed up dark hair, his sad blue eyes. His lush blue shirt, which he'd looked so good in last night, was all creased and half hanging out. He looked so confused and vulnerable. I just wanted to hug him and apologise.

"Oh that sounds like Georgina, always flying off the handle!" my mother's voice, broke through my thoughts like a spear in my brain.

I tensed up again to watch my mother take Ashley, as if a long lost relative offering him breakfast as if all the accusations of murder were never said. While she could carry on her favorite pastime slagging me off to anyone who had the time to listen.

"Oh she's always been thoughtless, she has caused nothing but trouble" I heard as I went back upstairs to get washed and dressed.

My Mam was on a roll now. I knew she would go on about my difficult birth and potty training etc. I've heard it all before and felt sorry for Ashley, but at least I knew I wouldn't see him again after this.

On return downstairs, I found my dad was dressed too.

"Let's get him home, eh" he said gently putting his arm around my shoulders.

"Sorry dad" I sighed.

I walked over to Ashley asked if he'd finished his breakfast, so that my dad and I could take him home. He sprung out of his chair while repeatedly, apologising and thanking my mother, he followed me out to my dad's car.

"Oh that's ok. I am sorry Georgina didn't even give you a blanket, you must have been freezing!" my mother cried out from the kitchen.

I got in the car in the front next to my dad, forcing Ashley to get in the back. Other than the directions Ashley gave my dad, we travelled in silence. Throughout the journey I held my head down in shame. I was so relieved when Ashley said we had arrived. I looked up as we pulled up outside a large detached mock Tudor house with double garage. *I thought how this would have dwarfed our Nans little miners cottage. It must have looked like a little hovel to him. I realised he was probably some rich spoiled kid, no wonder he was so well spoken. My pride in my working class background kicked in, that's why he assumed his luck was in. He probably thought I was his bit of rough, only being a daughter of an out of work coal miner.*

"Well Georgina?" my dad said breaking my angry thoughts.

"Oh yeah dad" I said getting out of the car. "Bye Ashley" I said shaking his hand. "Sorry about the confusion" I said resignedly while looking at my dad.

"That's ok, see you around, thanks for the lift Mr. Morgan" and off he went happily to his mansion.

"Not if I see you first, pillock!" I muttered under my breath while smiling and waving.

I went home to an angry Mam, disappointed Nan, quiet Dad and more rows. My Mam continued on the theme that I caused her nothing but trouble, unlike my brother and I was very close to being chucked out.

So here I am a bored sixth former not knowing what I want to do with my life, except I definitely need to leave home!

I snapped back to reality as I walked into Mr. Burke's office and took the phone receiver he offered. "Err ...Hello" I enquired.

"Hello is that Georgina Morgan? You don't know me, but my wife was apparently impressed with you when you worked for her for your work experience last summer" said a deep masculine welsh voice.

"Oh yes, Mrs. Williams the school dentist!" I replied excitedly. *Blimey I impressed someone!*

"Yes, well I have recently, err... lost my assistant at short notice and so I was wondering if you were still interested in becoming a dental surgery assistant. If you are, I could offer you a job. Perhaps we could get together for a chat to discuss it?"

"Wow! That would be great!" I exclaimed stunned "When?"

"Well let me see, what if you pop around my house about 8pm tonight?"

"Tonight!" I cried out before I could stop myself.

"I'm sorry, have you got more important plans for tonight?" he said with a hint of sarcasm in his voice.

"Err no... I think it will be alright? Could I have the address and phone number please?" I replied waving to Mr. Burke for a pen and paper which he hurriedly found for me. I took the details and then he was gone. I slumped into Mr. Burke's chair behind me in total disbelief.

"Well Georgina, Isn't that great, a job, well done!" Mr. Burke said whilst standing in front of me leaning on the desk beaming. I looked up confused, as I had forgotten he was there.

"Yes amazing!" I whispered just taking it all in.

"A job in this day and age. Your very lucky young lady!" he stated.

"So you think I should take it then?" I suddenly woke up, realizing I was in his chair. I awkwardly rose from his chair and walked towards the door. My careers teacher was almost pushing me out of his office. This was the guy that had once told our class that the high unemployment figures were due to women being able to work!

"Well you will have to discuss it with your parents, of course. This day and age you have to grab any opportunity you get. Let me know how you get on, bye" he said shutting the door in my face, I found myself in the corridor.

"Well thank you" I said under my breath and slowly make my way back to the sixth form common room.

"Alright Honey?" asked Sian as she put her arm protectively around me. I looked up at my friend's concerned face. Sian was a good friend, she always listened to me moaning about my Mam. Sian herself was fostered due to her mum dying during the birth of her baby sister. She was only about eight at the time and her alcoholic father couldn't look after them and put them both in care. Luckily, they were both fostered together and lived by me. This had left her very sensible and caring, she mothered everybody.

"You would never guess. I've only been offered a job!"

"A job!" her arm falling away as she took a step back.

"Yes as a dental surgery assistant!" I exclaimed.

"That's what you were thinking of doing when you left school wasn't it?"

"Yeah!" I said feeling better about it already. *Yes I had said that I wanted to be a dental surgery assistant after I went on work experience with the school dentist.*

"Fantastic! You jammy thing!" she cried giving me a big hug.

"Hey Julie have you heard this, Georgina's been offered a job!"

"Gosh that's brill!" she cried hugging me.

"Thanks mate!" I said as I was putting my dad's baggy black donkey jacket on while pushing my straight blonde shoulder length hair under my dad's old flat cap. My parents were used to me "borrowing" their clothes. My dad always said it always looked better on me anyway. I picked up my green canvass bag that I'd bought at the local Army and Navy store that I'd customized with arty graffiti of band logo's. Along with my doc martins boots, which I wore to death. To finish the ensemble I wore fingerless gloves. I suppose Sian and I were going through a grunge stage. Sian had dark brown hair, with a big flicking fringe, the back shaved short excepted for lots of tiny rats tails that were platted with different colored elastic bands with each one tied at the end . She also wore Doctor Martin boots and a red duffle coat. By the time we got to my Nan's house we had both decided that me leaving school would be cool!

I walked into my Nan's Cottage with a new found confidence, waving goodbye to Sian, as I closed the door.

I heard my Mam calling "Georgina! Is that you?"

"Yes" I sigh taking my coat off and hanging it up, waiting for the tirade to begin.

"Have you got any homework?" She asked.

"No" I call back as I sit on the stairs to remove my boots.

"Good" she says as she appears from the dining room and walks through to the living room. "You can sort out your stuff in Nan's room. She can't move about in her room with all your untidiness cluttering up the place! ...oh and by the way don't touch anything white!" just as I grabbed the banister to stand up.

"Arrgh! Mam why have you always got to be decorating!" I cry in disgust as I look at the white gloss paint sticking to my hand.

"You never fail! You always do it, don't you? You always have to touch the paint!" my mother yelled as she hurriedly gets the turps for me. Grabbing my hand so I won't do any further damage and dragged me into the kitchen. Like a flash, with experienced dexterity she was rubbing turps into my hand, while carrying on with her rant. I waited till she had finished. I think that my Mams way of coping with living at Nans is to keep herself busy and so she is decorating all the time.

"Mam I can't sort out Nan's room tonight! I've got an interview for a job tonight" I stated calmly.

"A job interview! Where?" Mam exclaimed releasing my hand.

"A local dentist wants a dental surgery assistant. Mrs. Williams the dentist, I did work experience with. You know the school dentist? Well she was so impressed with me, she told her husband and he has offered me a job. He wants to have at chat 8 o'clock tonight to discuss the details."

"You're going to his house?" she asked.

"Yes"

"Tonight!"

"Yes"

"You don't know him."

"No I don't?" I suddenly realised. I was so excited, I never questioned the details. "But I know his wife!" I said desperately.

"Sounds dodgy to me love "said Nan not looking up, as she sat knitting at the dining table.

"We will wait to see what your father says. What about you're A' levels?" My Mam tried to reason.

"We both know that the chances of me passing my exams are nil. I don't know what I'm doing there, I feel as I am just wasting my time."

It felt good to be honest at last and admit that I woke up every morning feeling a fraud. I was waiting for somebody to find me out and throw me out of the six form, I'd rather jump than be pushed.

"I am going to get showered and work out what I'm going to wear" I said feeling empowered. I turned and marched up stairs.

Right, what to wear? What do you wear for a "chat?" with your potential future boss I thought as I stood in my bedroom, wet from my shower and wrapped in a towel. Then I remembered I had a royal blue suit that I'd bought in the sale from Mam's catalogue. As I thought that by wearing a suit it would be easier for me to get served in pubs. So I wore the suit with a white shirt with a high collar with pearly buttons at the side of the neck. I eventually found a pair of tights that weren't laddered. I moussed, blow dried and tonged my hair to death, finishing off with loads of lacquer and a liberal spray of Charlie.

I walked downstairs to my brother's jeers "Where are you going sis, looking like an airhostess?"

"None of your business!" I say sticking my tongue out.

"Leave her alone she looks very nice!" our Mam said proudly while clipping Jack across the head with the tea towel.

"Thanks Mam" I reply glowing with her praise, it didn't happen often so I enjoyed it while it lasted.

"Tea's ready! Oh Georgina you shouldn't have put that blouse on now! You know what you're like with white!" she accused, with that she put her tea towel around my neck.

"Oh Mam! It smells of onions" I cry out.

"Leave it or you'll be sorry. Come on teas getting cold. I told your father your good news!" she shouted as she herded us into the dining room.

The kitchen come dining room was the heart of our house and Nan's was just the same. My dad and brother were already at the table with Nan. This is where we laughed, debated, putting all the world to right. Oh and we ate our food.

"So you have a job interview tonight then Georgie?" my dad said lightly.

"Glad that someone can get a job interview!" goaded Nan.

"Yeah" I said excitedly ignoring Nan, nothing was going to spoil this.

I hurriedly explained what had happened this afternoon.

"I know I haven't got any information but it was all so quick dad. I promise I will find out everything tonight dad. Oh and could you give me a lift please?"

"Yes of course. If you're sure you want to go?" my father said, concern showed in his pale blue eyes.

"Yes dad I need to do this. I'm dying of boredom in school" I pleaded. "Ok then that's sorted" my dad announced.

Printed in Great Britain
by Amazon